USTRATED CLASSICS

The Emperor's
New Clothes

The Three Hermits

The
Basilisk

Momotaro

Ali
Baba

Painted
Skin

Rama

David
and Goliath

OUND THE WORLD

STORIES
FROM AROUND THE WORLD

Library of Congress Cataloging in Publication Data

Stories from around the world

  (Illustrated classics)
    Contents: China: Painted Skin.—Africa: Hallabau's Jealousy.—
      Middle East: The Story of Ali Baba and the Forty Thieves. [etc.]
    1. Short stories. [1. Short stories. 2. Folklore] I. Stasiak,
    Krystyna, illus.

PZ5.S8818 [Fic] 74–1647

ISBN 0–8331–0031–9 (Regular Edition)
ISBN 0–8331–0032–7 (Deluxe Edition)

Illustrated Classics

STORIES FROM AROUND THE WORLD

Illustrated by
KRYSTYNA STASIAK

Edited & with an introduction by
MARGUERITE HENRY

Hubbard Press *Northbrook, Illinois*

Introduction
page 7

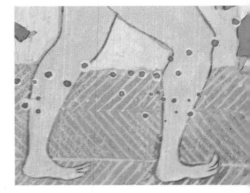

Stories

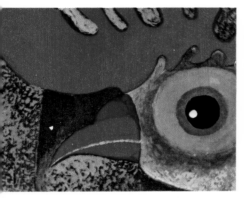

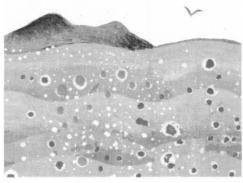
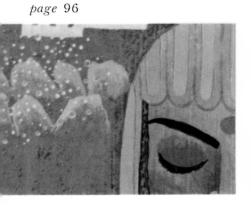
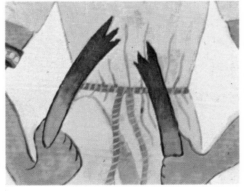

To fellow voyagers

who now face
daring adventures,
narrow escapes,
lusty fights,
giants on mountaintops,
hermits on islands,
monsters in caves,
and sages
who know all things
past, present, and future.

Introduction

MARGUERITE HENRY
*Author and
Newbery Award
winner*

Ever since my husband and I have lived in near-desert country, our refrigerator has held a glass jar labeled *Ali Baba's Nectar*. The crystalline liquid is really no more than boiled sugar and water, but we keep an ample supply on hand for a special ruby-throated hummingbird with an insatiable thirst.

We've named him Ali Baba because he hides in the topmost branches of a eucalyptus tree, where, unseen, he keeps a dawn-to-dusk watch on his constantly replenished feeder hanging outside our kitchen window. If an intruder so much as approaches his precious nectar, Ali Baba dives from his leaf-screened perch and sends the thief flying.

Imagine then my surprise and delight at seeing Krystyna Stasiak's illustration for "Ali Baba and the Forty Thieves." There, peeping out from his hideyhole in a treetop, sits Ali Baba, the woodcutter, watching the forty thieves on the ground below. It was like meeting an old friend!

Folk tales and legends have a way of inviting you to step through a looking glass into a whole other world. They implant themselves into your mind and marrow, ready to be called up whenever your mood needs brightening.

In this age of science fact and science fiction, it is fun and refreshing for a change to dip into pure fantasy—laughing again, walking hand in hand (or in paw) again with long-remembered companions. Was there ever, for example, such a cool and impudent cat as the schemer in that French tale "The Master Cat"? What other cat ever used his hunting skills to present plump rabbits and braces of partridge to grace a king's table? What other cat was ever a mentor to his master? And what other puss-in-boots became a lord with no further need to run after game—except for his own amusement? His ingenious tricks make you chuckle or laugh out loud, depending on how well you like cats.

If you prefer your heroes giant-sized and the nonsense lustier, then "Pecos Bill Meets Paul Bunyan" may be your favorite folk tale. Being a young country, America has few legendary heroes, but what it lacks in number is made up in prodigious toughness. Both Paul Bunyan and Pecos Bill were doughty pioneers, and both were ring-tailed roarers who changed the face of the United States. With one swing of his axe, Paul Bunyan gashed the earth—which accounts for the Grand Canyon. Pecos Bill, not to be outdone, swung his red-hot branding iron, and lo and behold we have the Painted Desert in Arizona.

In all folk tales, there is a solid understructure which gives a certain plausibility to the story—even with Pecos Bill and Paul Bunyan. In spite of their roaring and bragging and brawling, they respected each other as work giants in their fields: Paul as the first and strongest lumberjack in the world, and Pecos Bill who invented everything in the cattle business.

In this collection of folk stories some are sparely written, like a swift outline. Others are like a symphony; you think the tale has come to an end, with the villain conquered and the hero triumphant. Then suddenly the crash of music begins again and you are drawn into another unexpected movement.

Such a tale is "Mimer, the Master." It might have ended when the braggart of Burgundyland loses his head, or when the ninth son of King Volsung removes the sword implanted hilt-deep in the tree of life. But the total rightness and the poetic truths of the final melody would have been lost, and of the final words: "Siegfried sat alone before the smouldering fire and pondered upon what he had heard." Good stories never really end. They go on and on as long as the dreamer lives.

Each storyteller gives the same tale a different twist or turn, until the reader of more than one version is baffled. He bristles at change and prefers the way he first heard it, which may not be the original version at all.

No matter how improbable the stories are, somewhere along the line we catch glimpses of the culture and the nature of a people. In the story of "Little Burnt-Face" we might overlook the allegory. If read hurriedly, we may see only the Cinderella-like tale of the jealous sisters who hid little Burnt-Face at home while they went to meet the Great Chief. The Micmac Indians however saw in it something deeper. To them Little Burnt-Face symbolized the scorched face of the desert. The Great Chief was the rainbow who brought healing rain and washed the face of the desert into springtime bloom.

Nowhere in these myths does the storyline bog down with tedious description or sermonizing. The action is fast and the descriptions distilled to a nicety. We meet pompous people and humble ones; kindly kings and dastardly; thoughtful masters and resourceful servants; greedy grownups and children; and sharing, generous ones—like people we know. Like ourselves in a mirror?

Quite unaware of our good fortune, we gather, as we read, a harvest of riches to store and draw upon at odd times and in strange places. When we travel in Rome, the statues we see of a wolf suckling two boys will make us rejoice that the myth of Romulus and Remus still lives.

In Mexico we'll look upon the mountains of Popocatepetl and Ixtacihuatl and dream sadly of the Chichimec prince and the Toltec princess who were separated by a hopeless love.

But whether we travel or stay at home, we'll visit the lowlands of Germany, where Mimer guarded the well of wisdom; and Japan where ogres are "onis"; and Bethlehem to walk with the shepherd boy, David; and England with Galahad; and in China and in Nigeria, and Spain and India, we'll meet heroes who are resolute as the moon and the stars in their appointed rounds. No wavering whether "to be or not to be." They go forth and they accomplish.

In each legend we reach out for the meaty kernels of truth. In them is our sustenance, our security, and our dreams.

As Grandpa Beebe, down on Chincoteague Island, pointed out to his grandchildren: "Facts are fine fer as they go, but they're like waterbugs skittering atop the water. Legends, now—they go deep down and pull up the heart of a story."

Ali Baba

There lived in ancient times in Persia two brothers, one named Cassim, the other Ali Baba. Their father left them scarcely anything, but he divided equally the little property he had.

Cassim married a woman, who soon after became an heiress to a large sum of money and a warehouse full of rich goods, so that all at once he became a wealthy merchant and could live in ease.

Ali Baba, on the other hand, who had married a woman as poor as himself, lived in a wretched hut and maintained his wife and children by cutting wood, which he carried to town upon his three donkeys, and there sold.

One day when Ali Baba was in the forest and had cut wood enough to load his animals, he saw at a distance a great cloud of dust, and soon he could make out a troop of horsemen coming toward him. Fearing that they might be thieves, he turned loose his donkeys and climbed into a large tree, whose branches were so thick that he was completely hidden, while he himself could peep out without being discovered. The tree stood at the base of a steep rock, and there, at the foot of the rock, the horsemen dismounted.

Ali Baba counted forty in all. From their fierce looks and stealthy actions he suspected that they were thieves. Nor was he mistaken, for they were a roving band of robbers, who without doing any physical harm to people, carried off their treasures.

Every man unbridled and tethered his horse and hung about his neck a bag of corn. Then each of them lifted from his horse a saddlebag which, from its weight, seemed to Ali Baba to be full of gold and silver.

The captain of the band now made his way through the undergrowth and stood before the rock, directly under the tree in which Ali Baba sat hidden. Very distinctly he pronounced these words: "Open, Sesame." No sooner had he uttered the words than a door opened in the rock. In single file the captain made all his band enter before him. Then he followed, and the door shut of itself.

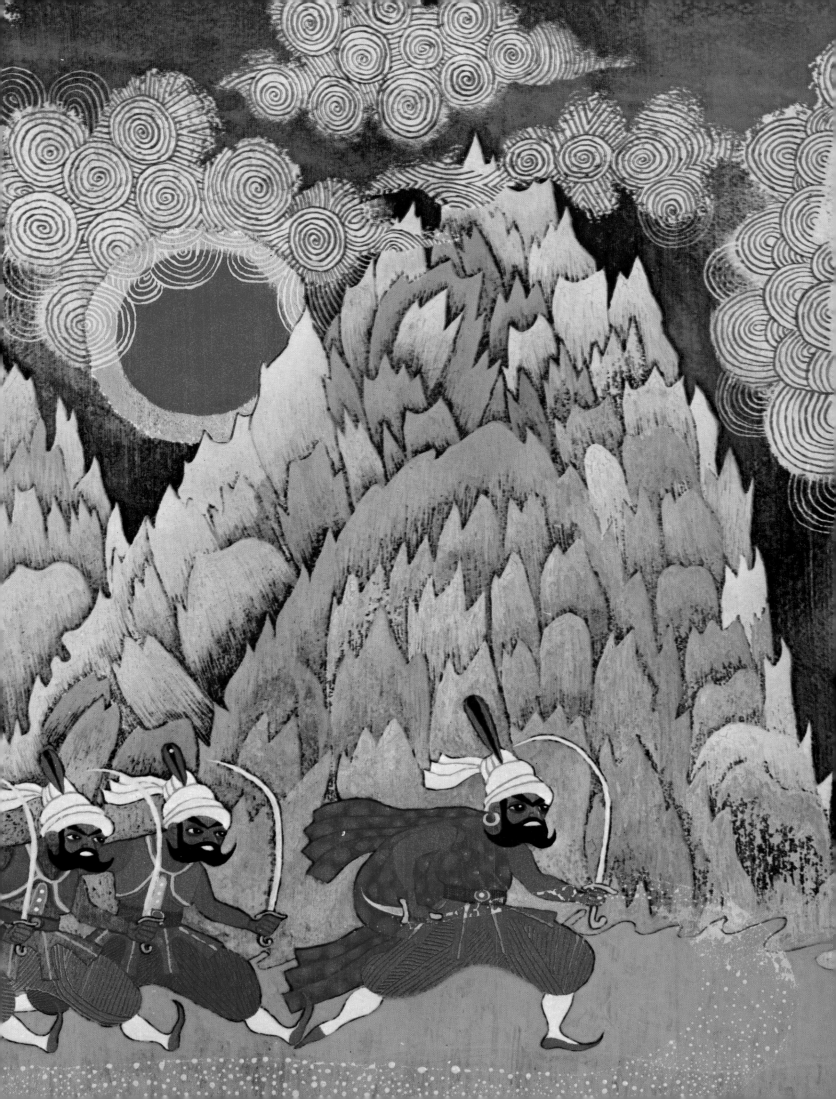

The robbers stayed some time within the rock. Meanwhile, Ali Baba—who feared that one of them might come out and catch him if he should try to escape—was obliged to sit patiently in the tree. At last the door opened again, and the forty robbers filed out. The captain came first and counted to see that all the others passed by him. When none of the thirty-nine was missing, he pronounced these words: "Shut, Sesame." Instantly the door of the rock closed again, as it was before.

With clocklike precision every man bridled his horse, fastened his empty saddlebag in place, and mounted. When the captain saw them all in readiness, he put himself at their head, and they returned by the way they had come.

Ali Baba did not immediately quit his tree. He followed the band of robbers with his eyes until they were out of sight. He then scrambled down, and remembering the words the robber-captain had used to cause the door to open and shut, he was filled with curiosity to see if his pronouncing them would have the same effect. Accordingly, he thrashed through the underbrush and stood before the closed door in the rock. In his biggest voice he said: "Open, Sesame." Instantly the door flew open.

To Ali Baba's astonishment, he found a spacious cavern in the form of a vault, which received adequate light from an opening in the top of the rock. The riches he could see from the threshold dazzled him. There were bales and bales of silk stuffs and brocades, and valuable carpeting piled in rolls one atop another, and gold and silver in ingots and in heaps, and a mound of bags probably filled with coins. The sight of all these riches made him suppose that the cave had been occupied for ages by bands of robbers who had succeeded one another.

Ali Baba took one step inside, and as soon as he did so the door shut of itself. This did not disturb him because he knew the secret with which to open it again. He paid no attention to the silver, but carried out much of the gold coin that was in bags. He collected his donkeys, which had strayed away, and when he had loaded them with the bags, he laid wood on top of them in such a manner that they could not be seen. Then he

stood before the door and pronounced the words: "Shut, Sesame." Soundlessly the door closed after him. He then made the best of his way to town.

When Ali Baba reached home, he drove his donkeys into a little yard, shut the gate carefully, threw off the wood that covered the bags, and carried them into the house, arranging them neatly before his wife. He then emptied the bags, which raised such a heap of gold as to stun her. Then from beginning to end he told her the whole of his adventure, and charged her to keep his secret.

The coins proved entirely too many to count in one night, so Ali Baba sent his wife out to borrow a small measure in the neighborhood. Away she ran to her brother-in-law, Cassim, who lived nearby, and asked his wife to lend her a measure for a little while. The sister-in-law did so, but as she knew of Ali Baba's poverty, she was curious to discover what sort of grain his wife wanted to measure. Artfully she smeared a film of suet in the bottom of the measure.

Ali Baba's wife went home, and through the long night helped her husband measure the heap of gold. Next day she carried the measure back again to her sister-in-law, but without noticing a paper-thin coin that had stuck to the bottom.

As soon as she was gone, Cassim's wife examined the measure. Her mouth fell agape to find a piece of gold stuck to it. "What?" said she. "Has Ali Baba gold so plentiful as to measure it? Where has that wretch got all his wealth?" Envy immediately rankled in her breast. Her husband was not at home, and she waited for his return with great impatience.

Cassim was scarcely in his house when his wife taunted: "Cassim! I know that thou thinkest thyself rich, but thou art mistaken. Ali Baba is infinitely richer. He does not *count* his money; he *measures* it!"

"Explain your riddle, wife."

In smug enjoyment, the wife told of her cleverness in greasing the measure with suet. Then she produced the paper-thin coin, which was so old they could not tell in what reign it had been coined.

Cassim, instead of being pleased, made no effort to conceal his envy of Ali Baba's prosperity. He could not sleep all that night for jealousy. In the morning he went to his brother before sunrise. "Ali Baba," said he, showing him the piece of money which his wife had given him, "thou pretendest to be miserably poor, and yet thou measurest gold! How many of these pieces hast thou? My wife found this at the bottom of the measure thou didst borrow yesterday."

Ali Baba, believing that Cassim and his wife knew all, told his brother, without showing the least surprise or trouble, by what chance he had discovered the hideaway of the thieves. He told him also in what place it was, and offered him part of his treasure to keep the secret.

"I expect an even amount," replied Cassim haughtily, "but I must know exactly where this treasure is, and how I may visit it myself when I choose. Otherwise, I will inform the Cadi, the civil judge, that thou hast this gold. Thou wilt then lose all thou hast, and I shall have a share for my information."

Ali Baba, more out of good nature than because he was frightened by the insulting menaces of his brother, revealed the location of the rock and taught him the very passwords to gain admission into the cave.

Cassim, who wanted no more of Ali Baba, left him, and immediately set out for the forest with his ten mules bearing great chests, which he designed to fill with treasure. He followed the road which Ali Baba had described, and before long reached the place by the tree and found the steep rock beside it.

When he discovered the entrance to the cave, he pronounced the words, "Open, Sesame." The door opened immediately, and no sooner had he entered than it closed silently behind him. To Cassim's surprise the cave held far more riches than he had dreamed. He could have spent the whole day feasting his eyes if the thought that he had come to carry off the treasures had not hindered him.

He laid as many bags of gold as he could carry at the door of the cavern, but his thoughts were so full of the great riches he would soon possess that he could not think of the words to make the door open. Instead of "Sesame," he said, "Open, Barley," and was much amazed to find that the door remained fast. He named several other grains, but still the door would not open, and the more he endeavored to remember the grain "Sesame," the more confounded he became. He threw down the bags of gold still in his arms and paced frantically up and down the cave, without the least interest in the riches that were around him.

About noon the robbers chanced to visit their cave, and at some distance saw Cassim's mules straggling about with great chests upon their backs. Alarmed, they galloped full speed to the cave, leaped from their horses, and while some searched about the rock, the captain and the rest went directly to the door, with their naked scimitars in their hands.

"Open, Sesame," the captain pronounced. Soundlessly the door opened. Cassim in a state of panic made a dash to escape, but the robbers with their scimitars soon deprived him of his life.

The next concern of the robbers was to examine the cache. They found all the bags which Cassim had piled by the door to load his mules, and they carried them again to their places, without missing what Ali Baba had taken before. Then, holding a council, they deliberated: How had this fellow gained entrance into their cave? They were aghast, for they had all been so sure that nobody knew their secret. It was a matter of utmost importance to them to secure their riches. They agreed, therefore, to cut Cassim's body into quarters and to hang two on one side and two on the other, within the door of the cave, in order to terrify anyone who might attempt to enter. They had no sooner taken this resolution than they put it into execution. They then left the place, closed the door, mounted their horses, and departed to attack any caravans they might meet.

In the meantime Cassim's wife became uneasy when darkness approached and her husband had not returned. She spent
the night in tears, and when morning came she ran to Ali Baba
in alarm. He did not wait for his sister-in-law to urge him to
see what had become of Cassim; he departed immediately with
his three donkeys, begging her first to hold her tears.

Pushing the animals to a fast pace, he went to the forest,
and when he came near the rock, he was seriously alarmed at
finding some blood spilt near the door. But when he pronounced
the words, "Open Sesame," and the door opened, he was struck
with horror at the sight of his brother killed and quartered.
He entered the cave, took down the remains, and having loaded
one of his donkeys with them, covered them over with wood.
The other two donkeys he loaded with bags of gold, covering
them with wood also. Then, bidding the door shut, he left the
cave.

Home before dusk, he drove the two donkeys loaded with
gold into his little yard, and left the care of unloading them to
his wife, while he led the other to his sister-in-law's house.

Ali Baba knocked at the door, which was opened by Morgiana, an intelligent servant whom Ali Baba knew to be faithful and resourceful in the most difficult situations. Taking
Morgiana aside, he said to her, "The first thing I ask of thee
is inviolable secrecy, which thou wilt find is necessary both
for thy mistress's sake and mine. Thy master's body is contained in these two bundles, and our business is to bury him as
though he had died a natural death. Go tell thy mistress that I
wish to speak to her, and mind what I have said to thee."

Morgiana went to her mistress, and Ali Baba followed her.
As kindly as he could, Ali Baba disclosed the incidents of his
journey and of Cassim's death. He endeavored to comfort the
widow, saying, "I offer to add the treasures which Allah hath
sent to me to what thou hast, and to marry thee, assuring thee
that my wife will not be jealous, and that we shall all be happy
together. If this proposal is agreeable to thee, I think that thou
mayest leave the management of Cassim's funeral to Morgiana,
thy faithful servant, and I will contribute all that lies in my
power to thy consolation."

What could Cassim's widow do but accept this merciful
offer? She therefore dried her tears, which had begun to flow

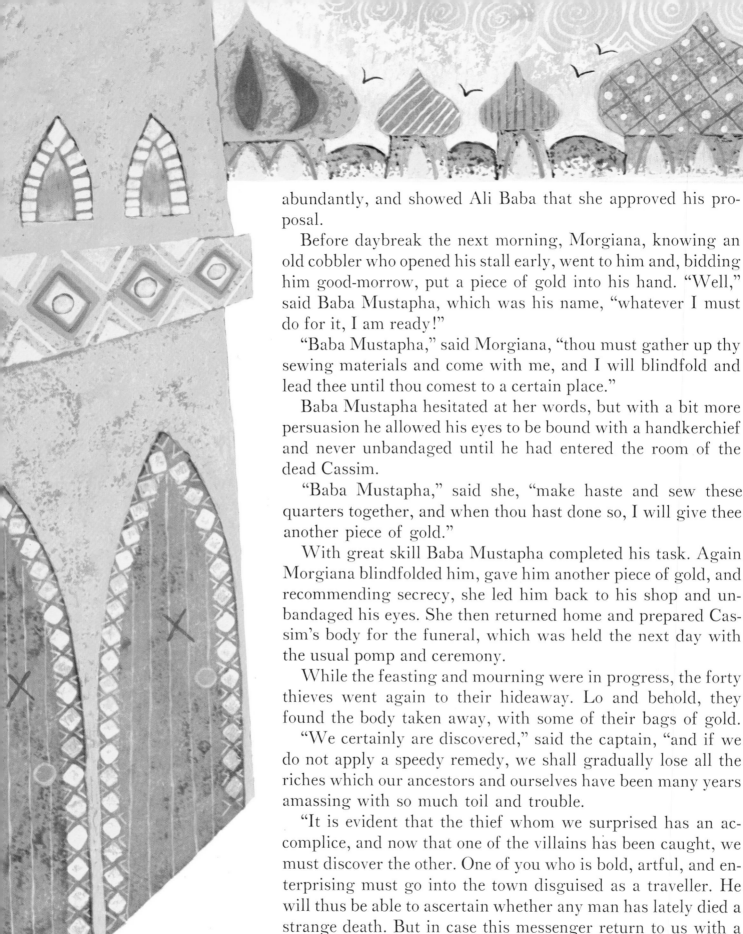

abundantly, and showed Ali Baba that she approved his proposal.

Before daybreak the next morning, Morgiana, knowing an old cobbler who opened his stall early, went to him and, bidding him good-morrow, put a piece of gold into his hand. "Well," said Baba Mustapha, which was his name, "whatever I must do for it, I am ready!"

"Baba Mustapha," said Morgiana, "thou must gather up thy sewing materials and come with me, and I will blindfold and lead thee until thou comest to a certain place."

Baba Mustapha hesitated at her words, but with a bit more persuasion he allowed his eyes to be bound with a handkerchief and never unbandaged until he had entered the room of the dead Cassim.

"Baba Mustapha," said she, "make haste and sew these quarters together, and when thou hast done so, I will give thee another piece of gold."

With great skill Baba Mustapha completed his task. Again Morgiana blindfolded him, gave him another piece of gold, and recommending secrecy, she led him back to his shop and unbandaged his eyes. She then returned home and prepared Cassim's body for the funeral, which was held the next day with the usual pomp and ceremony.

While the feasting and mourning were in progress, the forty thieves went again to their hideaway. Lo and behold, they found the body taken away, with some of their bags of gold.

"We certainly are discovered," said the captain, "and if we do not apply a speedy remedy, we shall gradually lose all the riches which our ancestors and ourselves have been many years amassing with so much toil and trouble.

"It is evident that the thief whom we surprised has an accomplice, and now that one of the villains has been caught, we must discover the other. One of you who is bold, artful, and enterprising must go into the town disguised as a traveller. He will thus be able to ascertain whether any man has lately died a strange death. But in case this messenger return to us with a false report, I shall ask you all if ye do not think that he should suffer death?"

All the robbers found the captain's proposal so fair that they unanimously approved it. Thereupon one of the robbers stood up and volunteered to be sent into the town. He received great praise from the captain and applause from his comrades.

Disguising himself next day and taking leave of the band, he went into the town, arriving just at sunup. He walked through the streets until quite by chance he came to Baba Mustapha's stall, which was open before any of the other shops.

The cobbler was seated with an awl in his hand. The robber saluted him, and noticing that he was quite old, said, "Honest man, thou beginnest work very early. Is it possible that one of thine age can see so well?"

"Certainly!" said Baba Mustapha. "Thou must be a stranger, or thou wouldst not ask. I have extraordinary eyes! Thou wilt not doubt it when I tell thee that I sewed a dead body together in a place where I had not so much light as I have now."

The robber was overjoyed at the information, and questioned Baba Mustapha until he learned all that had taken place. He then pulled out a piece of gold, and putting it into the cobbler's hand, said to him, "I can assure thee that I will never divulge thy secret. All that I ask is for thee to show me the house where thou didst thy stitching. Come, let me bind thine eyes as the servant girl bound them and we will walk on together. Perhaps thou mayest go direct to the house where thy mysterious adventure occurred. As everybody ought to be paid for his trouble, here is a second piece of gold for thee." So saying, he put another piece of gold into Baba Mustapha's hand.

The shining gold pieces were a great temptation to the cobbler. He looked at them for a long time without a word, thinking what he should do; but at last he pulled out his purse and dropped them inside. He then rose up, to the great glee of the robber, and said, "I do not assure thee that I shall be able to remember the way, but since thou desirest it I shall try."

The robber, who had his handkerchief ready, tied it over Baba Mustapha's eyes and walked by his side, partly leading him and partly guided by him.

"I think," said Baba Mustapha, "that I went no further than this," and he stopped before Cassim's house, where Ali Baba now lived.

Before the robber pulled off the bandage from the cobbler's eyes, he marked the door with a piece of chalk, which he had ready in his hand. Now that he could discover nothing more from Baba Mustapha, he thanked him for the trouble he had taken, and let him go back to his stall. In triumph, the robber rejoined his band in the forest and related his good fortune.

That same morning, a little after the robber and Baba Mustapha had departed, Morgiana went out of Ali Baba's house upon an errand. On her return she noticed the mark that the robber had made. "What does this sign forebode?" said she to herself. "Somebody means my master no good!" Without saying a word to her master or mistress, she fetched a piece of chalk and marked two or three doors on each side in the same manner.

Meanwhile the robber captain had armed his men, and was now addressing them: "Comrades," he said, "we have no time to lose. Let us set off for the town—only two at a time, to arouse no suspicion. I, as your captain, will go first with our clever comrade here who brought us the good news and found the scoundrel's house. We shall all rendezvous in the great square to decide our next course."

This speech and plan were approved by all, and soon they were paired off and ready to go. In parties of two each, they casually strolled into the town without being in the least suspected. The robber who had visited the town in the morning led the captain into the street where he had marked Ali Baba's residence, and when they came to the first of the houses, which Morgiana had marked, he pointed it out. But the captain observed that the next door was marked in the same manner. The robber became so confused that he had no explanation whatever to make. He was even more puzzled when he saw five or six houses similarly marked.

The captain, furious that their expedition had failed, went directly to the place of rendezvous and told the members of the band that all was lost, and that they must return at once to their cave. He himself set the example, and they all returned, two by two, as they had come.

When they were gathered together, at the rock, the captain told his comrades what had occurred, and the robber spy was

declared by all to be worthy of death. The spy condemned himself, acknowledging that he ought to have taken more precaution,
and he received with courage the stroke from him who was appointed to cut off his head.

The safety of the band seemed now more threatened than ever,
so another robber offered to go into the town and see what he
could discover. His offer being accepted, he went directly to the
shop of Baba Mustapha, gave him a gold piece, and was promptly
shown Ali Baba's house. When Baba Mustapha was glancing
elsewhere, the robber marked the house in a very inconspicuous
place. Not long after, Morgiana—whose eye nothing could escape
—went out and, seeing the new mark, she copied it in the same
place and in the same manner on the neighbors' houses.

On his return to the cave the second robber-spy reported his
adventure, and the captain and all the band were overjoyed at
the thought of immediate success. They went into the town with
the same precautions as before, but when the robber and his
captain came to the street where Ali Baba lived, they found a
number of houses marked alike, in the same inconspicuous spot.
At this the captain was enraged, and retired with his band to the
cave, where the second spy was condemned to death, and immediately beheaded.

Having lost two brave members of his band, and being afraid
lest he lose more, the captain resolved to take upon himself the
important mission. Accordingly, he went and addressed himself
to Baba Mustapha, who did him the same service he had done
for the other robbers. The captain did not mark the house with
chalk, but examined it so carefully that it was impossible for him
to mistake it. Well satisfied with his attempt, he returned to the
forest, and when he came to the cave, where the band awaited
him, he spoke:

"Now, comrades, nothing can prevent our full revenge. I am
certain of the house." He then ordered the members of the band
to go into the villages round about and buy nineteen mules and
thirty-eight large leathern jars, one full of oil and the others
empty.

In two or three days' time the robbers had purchased the mules
and the jars. The captain, after putting one of his men into each
jar, rubbed the outside of the vessels with oil. Things thus being
prepared, when the nineteen mules were loaded with the thirty-

seven robbers in jars and the jar of oil, the captain, as their driver set out for the town. He and his caravan arrived by the dusk of evening, as he had intended. He led the mules through the streets until he came to Ali Baba's house, at whose door he stopped.

Ali Baba was sitting there after supper to take a little fresh air, and the captain addressed him: "I have brought some oil a great distance to sell at to-morrow's market; it is now so late that I do not know where to lodge. If I should not be troublesome to thee, do me the favor to let me pass the night in thy house."

Though Ali Baba had seen the robber-captain in the forest and had heard him speak, it was impossible to know him in the disguise of an oil merchant.

"You shall be welcome," Ali Baba replied, and immediately opened wide his gates for the mules to pass through into the yard. At the same time, he called a servant and ordered him to fodder the mules. He then went to Morgiana to bid her prepare a good supper for his guest.

After supper the robber-captain withdrew to the yard, under the pretence of looking after his mules. Beginning at the first jar, and so on to the last, he said to each man, "As soon as I throw some stones out of my chamber window, cut the jar open with the knife which thou hast for that purpose, and come out. I will immediately join thee." Pleased at his plan, he returned to the house, and Morgiana, taking a light, conducted him to his chamber, where she left him.

Now Morgiana, returning to her kitchen, found that there was no oil in the house, and as her lamp was sputtering, she did not know what to do. Presently she bethought herself of the oil jars, and she went out into the yard. When she came nigh to the first jar, the robber within asked softly, "Is it time?" Though the robber spoke low, Morgiana heard him distinctly, for the captain, when he unloaded the mules, had taken the lids off the jars to give air to his men, who were ill at ease and needed room to breathe.

Morgiana was naturally surprised at finding a man in a jar instead of the oil she wanted, but she immediately comprehended the danger to Ali Baba and his family. Collecting herself, and without showing the least emotion, she answered, "Not yet, but presently." She went in this manner to all the jars, giving the same answer, until she came to the jar of oil.

By this means Morgiana found that her master, Ali Baba, who thought he was entertaining an oil merchant, had really admitted thirty-eight robbers into his compound. She made what haste she could to fill her oil pot, and returned to her kitchen. As soon as she had lighted her lamp, she took a huge kettle, went again to the oil jar, filled the kettle, and set it upon a freshly kindled woodfire. When the oil began to bubble and boil, she poured enough into every jar to scald and destroy the robber within. She then returned to her kitchen, put out the light, and resolved to stay awake by the window which opened into the yard.

She had not waited long before the robber captain gave the appointed signal by throwing little stones, several of which hit the jars. He then listened, and not hearing or seeing any movement among his companions, he became uneasy and descended softly into the yard. Going to the first jar, he smelt the boiled oil, which sent forth a steam and, examining the jars one after the other, he found all of his band dead. The last jar he examined was almost empty of oil, and immediately he guessed the means and manner of the death of his comrades.

Enraged to despair at having failed in his scheme, he forced the lock of a door that led from the yard to the garden, and climbing over the wall he made his escape.

Morgiana, satisfied and pleased to have succeeded so well in saving her master and his family, went to bed.

The next morning she took Ali Baba aside and told him of the sinister plan which had almost succeeded. Astonished beyond measure, Ali Baba examined all the jars, in each of which was a dead robber. He stood for some time motionless, now looking at the jars and now at Morgiana, without saying a word, so great was his gratitude. At last, when he had recovered himself, he spoke.

"I will not die," he said, "without rewarding thee as thou deservest! I owe my life to thee, and one day thou shalt have thy recompense, for I am convinced that the forty robbers had laid snares for my destruction. Allah, by thy means, hath delivered me from their wicked purpose, and I hope he will deliver all people from their persecution."

Ali Baba's garden was very long, and there he and his servants dug a pit in which they buried the robbers, and levelled the ground again. Ali Baba then returned to his house and hid the jars and weapons. The mules he sold in the market.

While Ali Baba was thus employed, the captain of the forty robbers returned to the forest and entered the cave. He sat there among his riches, determined to conjure up a new plot for avenging himself upon Ali Baba.

When he awoke early next morning, he disguised himself as a merchant, and, going into the town, took a lodging at an inn. He gradually carried from the cavern to the inn a great many rich stuffs and fine linens. He then took a shop opposite Cassim's warehouse, which Ali Baba's son had occupied since the death of his uncle. In less than a fortnight the pretended merchant had cultivated a friendship with the son, showering him with small presents, and asking him to dine and sup with him.

Ali Baba's son did not choose to be under such obligations to the pretended merchant. He therefore told his father that he would like in some way to return these kindnesses. Ali Baba, with great pleasure, took the entertainment upon himself, and invited his son to bring his new friend to supper. He then asked Morgiana to prepare a fine repast.

The pretended merchant accompanied the son to Ali Baba's home, and after the usual salutations said, "I beg of thee not to take it amiss that I do not remain for supper, for I eat nothing that has salt in it; therefore judge how I should feel at thy table!"

"If that be all," replied Ali Baba, "it ought not to deprive me of thy company at supper, for I promise thee that no salt shall be put in any meat served this night. Therefore, thou must do me the favor to remain."

Ali Baba then went into the kitchen and ordered that no salt be added to the meat that night. Morgiana, who was always ready to obey her master, was much dissatisfied at this peculiar order. "Who is this strange man," she asked, "who eats no salt in his meat? Does he not know that the eating of salt by host and guests cements for ever the bond of friendship?"

"Do not be angry, Morgiana," said Ali Baba. "He is an honest man; therefore kindly do as I bid."

Morgiana obeyed, though with reluctance. She was filled with curiosity to see this man who refused to eat salt with his host.

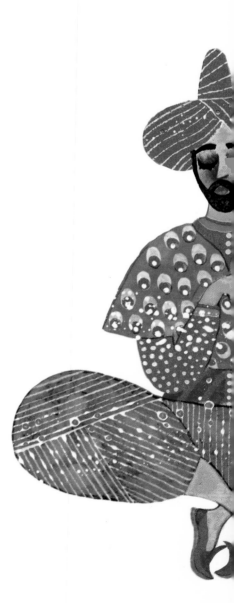

When she carried up the serving dishes, she studied the pretended merchant closely, and notwithstanding his disguise she knew for certain that he was the captain of the robber band. She also detected that under his garment he concealed a dagger.

Hastily Morgiana left the hall, and, retiring to her own chamber, dressed herself as a dancer, girding her waist with a silver sash, to which there hung a silver dagger. When she had thus clad herself, she said to a slave, "Take thy drum, and let us entertain our master and his son's guest."

The slave took his small drum and played all the way into the hall while Morgiana followed, whirling and pirouetting in such a manner as would have created admiration in any company.

After she had danced several numbers with charm and grace, Morgiana drew her dagger, and holding it in her hand began a difficult routine of leaping, thrusting movements. Sometimes she touched the dagger to her master's breast and sometimes to the son's, and oftentimes seemed to strike her own. At length she whirled toward the pretended merchant, and with a courage worthy of herself plunged the blade deep into his heart.

"Unhappy wench!" exclaimed Ali Baba. "What has thou done to ruin me and my family!"

"It was to *preserve*, not to ruin thee," answered Morgiana as she opened the robber's garment, showing his dagger.

"See what an enemy thou hast entertained! Look well at him, and thou wilt find both the false oil-merchant and the captain of the band of forty robbers. Remember, too, that he would eat no salt with thee. Wouldst thou have more to persuade thee of his wicked intentions?"

Ali Baba, overcome with emotion, embraced Morgiana and said, "Morgiana, I give thee thy liberty, and now I will marry thee to my son, who will consider himself fortunate to wed the savior of his family."

He then turned to his son, who readily consented to the marriage—not only because he wished to obey his father, but also because Morgiana was both beautiful and wise.

A few days later the nuptials were celebrated—first with solemnity, then with a sumptuous feast and dancing.

Afterward, Ali Baba took his son to the cave, and taught him its secret, which they in turn would hand down to their children's children. Meanwhile, however, they used their riches to do good, and they lived out their days in honor and comfort.

Little Burnt Face

Once upon a time, in a large Indian village on the border of a lake, there lived an old man who was a widower. He had three daughters. The eldest was jealous, cruel, deceitful, and ugly; the second was vain; but the youngest of all was gentle and fair.

Now, when the father was out hunting in the forest, the eldest daughter used to beat the youngest girl, and burn her face with hot coals until the people called her "Little Burnt-Face."

Each time the father came home from hunting he would ask why his youngest was so scarred, and the eldest would answer quickly: "She is a good-for-nothing! She was forbidden to go near the fire, and she disobeyed and fell in." Then the father would scold Little Burnt-Face and she would creep away to cry herself to sleep.

On the other side of the lake, in a beautiful wigwam at the end of the village, lived a Great Chief who had the power to make himself invisible. In fact, no one had ever seen him but his sister —to whom he was very kind. He brought her many deer and supplied her with good things to eat from forest and lake. He also provided her with the finest blankets and garments.

When visitors came to the wigwam, all they ever saw of the Chief were his moccasins; for when he took them off they became visible, and his sister hung them up.

Now, one spring, his sister made known that her brother, the Great Chief, would marry any maiden who could see him.

All the girls from the village—except Little Burnt-Face and her sisters—and all the girls for miles around hastened to the wigwam and walked along the shore of the lake, hoping to see their future husband. Instead, they saw only the Chief's sister who asked:

"Do you see my brother?"

Some of them said, "No"; but most answered, "Yes."

Then his sister asked, "Of what is his shoulder-strap made?"

And the girls said, "Of a strip of rawhide."

"And with what does he draw his sled?"

And they replied, "With a green withe."

Then the sister knew they had not seen him at all, and she said quietly, "Let us go to the wigwam."

So to the wigwam they went, and when they entered, they were told not to take the seat next the door, for that was where the Chief sat.

Eagerly the girls helped cook the supper, for they were very curious to see the Great Chief eat. When all was ready and served on the Chief's plate, the food quickly disappeared. Then the brother took off his moccasins, and his sister hung them up. But the girls never saw the Chief, though many of them stayed all night.

One day the two sisters of Little Burnt-Face put on their finest blankets and brightest beads. They plaited their hair neatly, and slipped embroidered moccasins on their feet. Then they started out to see the Great Chief.

As soon as they were gone, Little Burnt-Face made herself a dress of white birch bark and a cap and leggings of the same. She threw off her ragged garments, and dressed herself in her birch bark clothes. She put her father's moccasins on her bare feet; and the moccasins were so big that they came nearly to her knees. Then she, too, started out to visit the Great Chief in the beautiful wigwam at the end of the village.

Poor Little Burnt-Face was a sorry sight! Her hair was singed off, and her small face was as full of scars as a sieve is full of holes. She shuffled along in her father's big moccasins, and as she passed through the village, the boys and girls hooted at her.

When she reached the lake, her sisters saw her coming and tried to shame her. "Go back home!" they cried out. But the Great Chief's sister received her kindly, and bade her stay, for she saw the gentleness of Little Burnt-Face.

As evening was coming on, the four girls went walking beside the lake. Suddenly the sky grew quite dark, and they all sensed that the Great Chief had come.

His sister turned to the two elder girls. "Do you see my brother?"

And they said, "Yes."

"Of what is his shoulder-strap made?"

"Of a strip of rawhide," they replied, for that was what their father wore.

"And with what does he draw his sled?"

And the girls said, "With a green withe."

Then his sister turned to Little Burnt-Face and asked, "Do you see him?"

"I do! I do!" said Little Burnt-Face in awe. "And he is wonderful!"

"Of what is his sled-string made?" asked his sister.

"It is a rainbow!" cried Little Burnt-Face.

"Of what is his bow-string made?"

"His bow-string," replied Little Burnt-Face, "is the Milky Way!"

Then the Great Chief's sister smiled with delight, and taking Little Burnt-Face by the hand, she said, "You have surely seen him."

She led the little girl to the wigwam, and bathed her with dew until the burns and scars disappeared. Her skin became soft and lovely again. Her hair grew long, and it shone like the blackbird's wing. Then his sister brought from her treasures a wedding-garment, and she dressed Little Burnt-Face in it. And she was most beautiful to behold.

After all this was done, his sister led the little girl to the seat next the door, saying, "This is the Bride's seat," and made her sit down.

And then the Great Chief, no longer invisible, entered, terrible and beautiful. And when he saw Little Burnt-Face, he smiled and said gently, "So we have found each other!"

And she answered, "Yes."

Then Little Burnt-Face was married to the Great Chief, and the wedding-feast lasted for days, and to it came all the people of the village. As for the two bad sisters, they went back to their wigwam in disgrace, weeping with shame.

The Emperor's New Clothes

Many years ago there lived an emperor who thought so much of fine clothes that he spent all his money in order to be elegantly dressed for every occasion. He cared nothing for his soldiers, nor for going to the play; or driving in the park—except to show his new clothes. He had a coat for every hour of the day, and just as they say of a king, "He is in the council-room," so they always said of him, "The Emperor is in his dressing-room."

The city where he lived was famous for its gaiety. Travelers of every description flocked there. One day there came two swindlers; they posed as weavers, and boasted they could weave the finest cloth to be imagined. Their colors and patterns, they said, were not only exceptionally beautiful, but clothes made of their material possessed the magical quality of being invisible to any man who was unfit for his office or hopelessly stupid.

"Aha!" said the Emperor. "If I wore such clothes, I should be able to find out which men in my empire were unfit for their places, and I could tell the clever from the stupid. Yes, I must have this cloth woven for me without delay." And he gave a bag of money to the two swindlers in advance, so that they should set to work at once.

In great glee the two men set up two looms, and pretended to be very hard at work, but they had nothing whatever on the looms. They asked for the finest silk and the most precious gold; this they put in their own bags, and worked at the empty looms till late into the night.

"I should very much like to know how they are getting on with their weaving," thought the Emperor. But he felt rather uneasy when he remembered that he who was not fit for his office could not see the cloth. He believed, of course, that he had nothing to fear for himself, so he thought he would send somebody else to see how matters stood. Everybody in the town had been told what a wonderful property the stuff possessed, and all were anxious to see how stupid or how unworthy of office their neighbors were.

"I will send my honest old Minister of State to the weavers," thought the Emperor. "He can judge best how the stuff looks, for he is intelligent, and nobody understands his office better than he."

So the good old Minister went into the room where the two swindlers sat working at the empty looms. "Heaven preserve us!"

he thought, and opened his eyes wide. "I cannot see anything at all," but he did not say so. Both swindlers bade him be so good as to come close to the looms in order to admire the exquisite pattern and the beautiful colors. The poor Minister opened his eyes wider, but he could see nothing, for there was nothing to be seen. "Good Lord!" he thought, "can I be that stupid? I should never have thought so, and nobody must know! Or is it possible that I am unfit for my office? No, no, I can never report that I was unable to see the cloth."

"Well? Have you nothing to say?" asked the first swindler as he picked up his shuttle.

"Oh, it is very pretty—quite enchanting!" said the old Minister, peering through his spectacles. "What a pattern, and what colors! I shall tell the Emperor I am very much impressed."

"We are glad of that," replied both the weavers, and they named the colors to him and explained the curious pattern. The Minister listened attentively, then hastened to the Emperor to report the information in great detail.

Immediately the swindlers asked for more silk and more gold for their weaving. They kept it all for themselves; not a thread came near the looms. Yet they continued, as hitherto, to work at the empty looms.

Soon afterward the Emperor sent another honest courtier to the weavers to see how they were getting on, and if the cloth was nearly finished. Like the old Minister, he looked and looked, but could see nothing, as there was nothing to be seen.

"Is it not a beautiful piece of cloth?" asked the two swindlers, showing and explaining the magnificent pattern which, however, was not there at all.

"I am *not* stupid," thought the man. "Is it therefore my high office for which I am not fit? If so, I must not let anyone know it." He therefore praised the cloth, which he did not see, and expressed his pleasure at the beautiful colors and the fine pattern.

"Yes, it is quite enchanting," said he to the Emperor.

By now everybody in the whole city was talking about the resplendent cloth. At last the Emperor wished to see it himself while it was still on the loom. With a whole company of chosen men, including the two honest councillors who had already been there, he went to the two swindlers, who were now weaving as hard as they could, without any thread.

"Is it not magnifique?" said the old Minister and the first courtier in unison. "Will your Majesty see what a pattern and what colors?" And they pointed to the empty looms, for they imagined the others could see the cloth.

"What is this?" thought the Emperor.."I do not see anything at all. This is terrible! Am I stupid? Am I unfit to be emperor? That would indeed be the most dreadful thing that could happen to me."

Taking a deep breath and summoning all his dignity, he said, "Yes, it is very fine; it has our highest approval." He stood gazing at the empty loom, nodding his consent for he did not like to say he could see nothing. His attendants, too, looked and looked, and although they could see no more than the others, they said, like the Emperor, "It is very fine." And all advised him to wear the new clothes at a great procession which was soon to take place.

"Magnifique! Beautiful! Excellent!" The words went from mouth to mouth. Everybody seemed so delighted that the Emperor knighted each of the swindlers and conferred upon them the title of Imperial Court Weavers.

All through the night before the procession, sixteen candles were kept burning in the room of the looms. People could see that the weavers were busily getting the Emperor's new clothes ready. They pretended to take the cloth from the loom. They snipped the air with big scissors. They sewed with needles without thread. And at last they said, "Now, the Emperor's new clothes await his royal person."

The Emperor, with all his noblest courtiers, then came in. They watched in eagerness as the swindlers each held an arm outstretched as if displaying something. One said, "See, here are the trousers! Here is the coat!" The other said, "Here is the cloak! See how light they are—like a cobweb! They make one feel as if one had nothing on at all, but that is the beauty of it."

"Yes," said all the courtiers; but they could not see anything, for there was nothing to be seen.

"Will it please your Majesty graciously to take off your clothes?" said the swindlers. "Then we may help your Majesty into the new clothes before the large looking-glass!"

The Emperor took off all his clothes, and the swindlers pretended to put the new clothes upon him, one piece after another. The Emperor looked at himself in the glass from every side.

"Oh, how well they look! How well they fit!" said all. "What a pattern! What colors! What style!"

"Your Majesty," said the chief master of the ceremonies, "your lackeys are waiting outside with the canopy which is to be borne over your Majesty in the procession."

"I am quite ready," said the Emperor. "Does not my suit fit me marvellously?" He turned once more to the looking-glass, that people should think he admired his garments.

The chamberlains, who were to carry the train, fumbled with their hands on the ground as if lifting up a train. Then they pretended to hold up something in their hands; they dared not let people know that they held nothing at all.

And so the Emperor marched in the procession under the beautiful canopy, and all who saw him from the roadside or from out of their windows exclaimed, "How marvellous is the Emperor's new suit! What a long train he has! How perfect the fit!" Nobody would let others know that he saw nothing, for then he would have been unfit for his office or too stupid. Never before had the Emperor's clothes been such a success.

"But he has nothing on at all," said a little child.

"Good heavens! Hear what the little innocent says!" said the father. Then nearby spectators began whispering, each to the other, "A little child says he has nothing on at all!"

"He has nothing on at all!" cried all the people at last. And the Emperor too was feeling much worried, for it seemed to him that they were right, but he thought to himself, "All the same, I must keep the procession going now." So he held himself stiffer than ever, and the chamberlains walked on and held up the train which was not there at all.

The Basilisk

Once upon a time, the people of Warsaw used to tell of a Basilisk who lived in the cellar of the King's mansion. This creature guarded treasures, rich and rare, and no one, not even the King, could get near them. It was not known how the Basilisk came to be there, and the King promised 500 gold coins to anyone who could destroy this strange and frightful creature. He had the head of a rooster topped with a great red comb. His long neck coiled like a snake and was covered with silvery scales. His body was covered with black feathers, and his strong legs had long claws. But most terrible of all were the creature's eyes—large and round and glowing with a thousand colors. These eyes had great power—power to kill anyone upon whom the Basilisk looked.

The cellar where the Basilisk lived was murky and mysterious. Everything was covered with a mossy mold and laced with silvery cobwebs. A narrow stone stairway led down to the cellar, jagged and slick from dampness. Any sound or footstep echoed far into the gloom of the old walls. The treasures were hidden in great moldy chests bound in metal and locked with very large keys made of brass. Day and night, the Basilisk stood guard over them, and if anyone dared to enter, he killed them with his terrible eyes.

A great warrior, Sir Castelan, was planning to destroy the Basilisk. A great sword and suit of armor were being forged for Sir Castelan by the master blacksmith, Martin. One day, as Master Martin encouraged his journeymen to work harder, his beautiful twin children, Jan and Anna, came to the forge and watched the painstaking labor. They, too, were excited that soon another warrior would try to destroy the terrible Basilisk. But Jan and Anna soon grew tired of watching the huge bellows fan the fire and listening to the loud hammering of the forge. They asked their father if they might go to the Old Town Market. Because he was so very busy, he quickly consented, but sternly warned they must not go near the King's mansion, which was near the gay, colorful market.

Jan and Anna loved to see the brightly festooned booths with the beautiful dolls, toys, and richly embroidered fabrics for sale. The children's eyes grew wide with wonder as they watched trained monkeys dance on a rope, and a great lion leap through a flaming hoop. Before they knew it, they had wandered near the old mansion where the Basilisk guarded the treasures. Remembering her father's warning Anna became frightened, but Jan was unafraid and curious to see the monster lurking in the mysterious cellar. Anna, taking her brother's hand, pleaded and pleaded with him to leave. But Jan persuaded her that they should take one little look and then hurry home.

They pushed the great brass door open just a crack, squeezed through, and crept silently down the slimy stone steps. The closer they came to the bottom, the more frightened they became. Overhead, gloomy bats rustled their wings, and owls stared with great shining eyes. A tiny window covered with ancient dust and cobwebs let a greenish light into the murky cellar. Suddenly, the frightened children saw the back of the Basilisk and darted quickly behind an old chest. The terrible creature heard the sound. Ruffling his hideous feathers, he turned his rooster-head and looked upon the staircase with his flashing eyes. The children squeezed far down behind the chest, clinging to each other in fright, and the Basilisk did not see them. He did not move, thinking the noise was made by an owl or a bat.

Meanwhile, the parents became upset that the children had not returned home and started searching through the market, calling loudly. Jan and Ann could hear the calls, but they didn't dare answer them.

After searching the town, Martin and his wife realized where the children had gone. Panic-stricken, they hurried to seek the advice of a graybearded old sage who had dozens of books of wisdom, and who could find a solution for any problem. They told him of their children's misfortune and asked for his help. The old sage pondered, shook his head, and said that there was a way to rescue the children—a very difficult and a very dangerous way. It was necessary, he said, for someone to shield himself with many mirrors and then to go down into the cellar and confront the Basilisk. When the Basilisk looked into the mirrors and saw his own reflection, he would die from his own piercing look. This was the only way, said the sage, that the children could be saved and the town freed from the dreadful creature.

Even the thought of such an act alarmed the blacksmith's wife, and she began to cry. Master Martin, although he was terribly frightened, decided that he himself would go down into the terrible cellar. Quickly Martin and his wife ran to the market and bought four very large mirrors. Then they went to the church and prayed fervently to God that the mission might succeed, and that the children and the blacksmith would be saved.

Hanging the mirrors all about himself, Master Martin embraced his wife. With tears in his eyes, he hurried toward the fearful cellar. A crowd gathered outside the old mansion, and the people whispered among themselves fearfully. Martin's wife whispered prayers continually, and the blacksmith blessed himself as he stepped across the threshold of the brass-bound door.

As he descended the steps slowly, the mirrors tinkled. Once again the Basilisk turned his glowing eyes toward the stairs.

Suddenly, the Basilisk shrieked horribly, like the crowing of a rooster, the hissing of a snake, and the laughter of a devil—all at the same time. The crowd outside trembled. The blacksmith's heart froze. The children clung to one another even more tightly.

Then all was still.

When the children dared to peek from behind the chest, they saw that the Basilisk lay lifeless on the ground, killed by the reflection of his own terrible eyes.

The children rushed to their father's arms, crying and pleading for his forgiveness, promising never to disobey again. When the King learned about the brave blacksmith who had saved the lives of his children and freed the townspeople from the dreadful Basilisk, he presented Master Martin with the reward of 500 shiny gold coins.

The blacksmith lived in peace and prosperity forever after, and the King had his treasures to himself in the old mansion the people of Warsaw still call "The Basilisk Mansion."

The Love of a Mexican Prince and Princess

Among the ancient Toltecs of Mexico there was once a king who had a daughter as regal as a lily. So many fine noblemen courted her that she could not decide which one to marry. The years passed, and she was still unmarried.

One day there came to the capital city of Teotihuacan a Chichimec prince, to buy and to trade. He arrived on a golden litter, dressed in colored robes and adorned with brilliant feathers. Many warriors accompanied him, as was befitting a prince. But the Toltecs looked down on the Chichimec people, who lived in the far Ajusto mountains, hunting and fishing. They had little to do with them, calling them the dog people.

As was his habit, the prince and his followers went to the market place, examining blankets, animals, carvings, and golden ornaments. On that very day the beautiful Toltec princess was also in the market, buying embroideries and woven baskets and colored blankets for her palace. The prince and the princess met quite by accident, and suddenly it seemed to both of them that the sun was shining more brightly and the birds in their cages were singing more sweetly. Each felt a quickening of love for the other, though each knew this was a forbidden and hopeless dream. A Toltec princess could marry only a man of her class among the Toltecs. Similarly, a Chichimec prince could select his bride only from among his equals in the Chichimec nation. Such were the laws of their lands.

But love makes its own laws. The prince and princess felt that life would not be worth living without each other.

The maidens who accompanied the princess saw the longing in her eyes and understood. But they, too, knew the edict of their people and of the Chichimecs, so they hurried the princess back to her palace.

The prince with his attendants also returned to his home. He burned with anger at the thought that he could not be with the Toltec princess. He tried to put her out of his mind, but he could not.

One morning he dressed with a shining leopard skin about his shoulders, and around his loins a cloth woven of the finest maguey fibers. On his arms and about his neck he wore jewels of jade and precious stones, and on his head he set a gleaming headdress of green quetzal feathers. Thus arrayed, he set out with his followers and came again to the great capital of Teotihuacan, where he wandered about, close to the palace of the king.

It was not long before the princess knew he was there, and she left the palace, adorned in rich white lace. Her glossy black hair hung down from her proud head in graceful braids bound in colored bands and jewels.

The prince and princess met and spoke in secret. The prince vowed he would come for her shortly and take her to be his wife.

Soon messengers of the Chichimec prince arrived at the Toltec court. On behalf of the prince, they asked the king for the hand of his daughter in marriage.

The king grew livid with fury. "My daughter will marry only a Toltec noble, never a Chichimec beneath her station!"

The messengers bore this unyielding verdict to their master, while the angry king hid his daughter away where she could see no one. But the princess was attended by a maid who believed the king's course of action was unjust. She willingly carried a note to the prince, telling him where to meet the princess as soon as she was released.

When the king thought his daughter had forgotten the prince, he set her free. Losing no time, she hurried to the meeting place in the woods, and the two lovers went up into the mountains together, planning their future.

The next day the princess returned and revealed to her father that she and the Chichimec prince were married.

"Please forgive me, my father, I know that our custom forbids me to marry a Chichimec, but I love him, and for me love is greater than custom."

When the king heard this, he was angry beyond words.

"Get out of my sight!" he cried. "You have brought shame upon me. I banish you, and I forbid any Toltec to give food and shelter to either of you. May wild animals devour you both!" Heartbroken, the princess left the palace.

Almost the same words were spoken to the prince. His father, too, felt that his son had greatly shamed him by marrying outside his own people, and he forbade any Chichimec to give food or shelter to him or his wife.

Exiled from their homes, the prince and princess set out on their life of wandering. Through mountains and valleys, over rivers and streams they went, and no Toltec nor Chichimec offered them food or shelter. They lived only on herbs and wild berries, for the prince had no weapons with which to hunt. Cold winds came, and the two outcasts began to lose their strength. But as their bodies grew weaker, their love grew stronger.

One night they took refuge in a little valley from which they could see the proud capital of Teotihuacan. A mountain rose on either side of the valley. The wind grew bitter and a whirl of snow swept into their shelter. The prince could feel that the princess was thinking of her home.

"My princess," said he, "we chose love above life, so life is not important to us. The snows of winter will soon imprison us. No one wants us. We cannot rest anywhere. Soon we shall be so cold that we shall die. Let this be our last night in the lands where we are not wanted. Tomorrow shall we part and enter the world of spirits, where there is no difference between Toltec and Chichimec. Here we committed a crime against our peoples. In the other world there is only one people, and all live together in peace."

A silence crept in while snowflakes spattered their hair and eyelashes. "Tomorrow," the prince said, "you go to the lower mountain that watches over your city, and I shall go to the higher mountain that also watches over your city. On top of these mountains your body and mine will find resting places. I shall watch over you, and our spirits will become one."

The princess knew that her husband had spoken with divine wisdom.

In each other's arms they spent their last night. When the red sun rose above the mountains, they bade each other farewell. Then each turned toward the appointed mountain and began to climb. The princess went up Ixtaccihuatl mountain, climbing slowly, while the icy wind blew and the snow fell over her. When at last she reached the top, she lay down, her eyes staring fixedly at the sky.

The snow kept falling, slowly, softly, and soon mounded over her body in a tufted white blanket.

Always, to this day, a swirl of snow crowns the peak of Ixtaccihuatl, protecting the princess from the biting cold winds.

The prince also climbed his mountain, and when he reached the top he, too, lay down and was covered by the thick snow.

After a time, smoke came out of the mountain, and the bowels of the earth grumbled and growled. The people called it "Smoky Mountain," or Popocatepetl. It is said that the smoke and the grumbling are caused by the Chichimec prince crying for his Toltec princess.

The Three Hermits

A bishop was sailing from Archangel to the Solovetsk Monastery, and on the same vessel were a number of pilgrims on their way to visit the shrines there. The voyage was a smooth one. The wind favorable and the weather fair. The pilgrims aboard sat on deck, eating in groups, talking to one another. The Bishop, too, came on deck, and as he was pacing up and down, he noticed a huddle of men standing near the prow, listening to a fisherman who was excitedly talking and pointing far out to sea. The Bishop stopped and looked in the direction in which the man was pointing. He, however, could see nothing but rippling waves glistening in the sunshine. He drew nearer, but when the fisherman saw him, he took off his cap and was silent. The rest of the people also took off their caps and bowed.

"Do not let me disturb you, friends," said the Bishop. "I came to hear what this good man is saying."

"The fisherman was telling us about the hermits," replied one, a tradesman, rather bolder than the rest.

"What hermits?" asked the Bishop, going to the side of the vessel and seating himself on a box. "Tell me about them. I should like to hear. What were you pointing at?"

"Why, that little island you can just see over there," answered the man, pointing to a spot ahead and a little to the right. "That is the island where the hermits live for the salvation of their souls."

"Where is the island?" asked the Bishop. "I see nothing."

"There, in the distance, if you will please look along my hand. Do you see that little cloud? Below it, and a bit to the left, there is just a faint streak. That is the island."

The Bishop looked carefully, but his unaccustomed eyes could make out nothing but the water shimmering in the sun.

"I cannot see it," he said. "But who are the hermits?"

"They are holy men," answered the fisherman. "I had long heard tell of them, but never chanced to see them myself till the year before last when, on a wild stormy night, my boat capsized in the lee of their island. I knew not where I was. In the morning I wandered about and came to an earth hut. An old man stood near it. Presently two others came out. They kindly dried my clothes, fed me, and helped me mend my boat."

"And what are they like?" asked the Bishop.

"One is a small man who wears a priest's cassock. He is humped over and is very old; he must be more than a hundred, I should say. He is so old that the white of his beard is taking a greenish tinge, but he is always smiling, and his face is as bright as an angel's from heaven. The second is taller, but he also is very old. He wears a tattered peasant coat. His beard is broad and of a yellowish gray color. He is a strong man. Before I had time to help him, he turned my boat over as if it were only a pail. He, too, is kindly and cheerful. The third is tall, and has a beard as white as snow, reaching to his knees. He is stern, with over-hanging eyebrows. He wears nothing but a piece of matting tied round his waist."

"And did they speak to you?" asked the Bishop.

"For the most part they did everything in silence. They spoke but little, even to each other. One of them would just give a glance, and the others would understand him. I asked the tallest whether they had lived there long. He frowned and muttered something as if he were angry; but the oldest one took his hand and smiled, and then the tall one was quiet. The oldest one only said: 'Have mercy upon us,' and smiled."

While the fisherman was talking, the ship had drawn nearer to the island.

"There! Now you can see it plainly, if your Lordship will focus in this direction," said the tradesman, pointing with a gnarled finger.

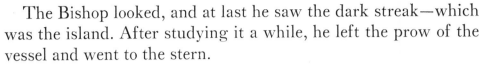

The Bishop looked, and at last he saw the dark streak—which was the island. After studying it a while, he left the prow of the vessel and went to the stern.

"What island is that?" he asked the helmsman.

"It has no name," replied the man. "There are many such in this sea."

"Is it true that hermits live there for the salvation of their souls?"

"So it is said, your Lordship, but I don't know if it's true. Fishermen say they have seen them; but of course they may only be spinning yarns."

"I should like to land on the island and see these men," said the Bishop. "How could I manage it?"

"The ship cannot get close to the island," replied the helmsman, "but you might be rowed there in a boat. You had better speak to the captain."

The captain was sent for and came.

"I should very much like to see the hermits on that island," said the Bishop. "Could I not be rowed ashore?"

The captain tried at first to dissuade him.

"Of course it could be done," said he, "but we should lose much time. And if I might venture to say so, your Lordship, the old men who live there are not worth your pains. I have heard that they are foolish old fellows, who understand nothing, and never speak a word, any more than the fish in the sea."

"I wish to see them," said the Bishop, "and I will pay you for your trouble and loss of time. Grant me the use of a boat."

There was no discouraging the Bishop; so the order was given. The sailors trimmed the sails, the steersman put up the helm, and the ship's course was set for the island. A chair was placed at the prow for the Bishop, and he sat there, looking ahead. The pilgrims and the crew who had the sharpest eyes could presently make out the rocks on the island, and then a mud hut. At last one man saw the hermits themselves. The captain brought a telescope, and after looking through it, handed it to the Bishop, saying:

"Good enough! I count three men there, a little to the right of that big rock."

The Bishop took the telescope, got it into position, and he too saw the three men: a tall one, a shorter one, and one very small and bent. They were standing on the shore, holding each other by the hand.

The captain turned to the Bishop.

"The vessel can get no nearer than this, your Lordship. If you wish to go ashore, we must ask you to go in the dinghy, while we anchor here."

The cable was quickly let out, the anchor cast, and the sails furled. There was a jerk, and every timber in the vessel shook. Then, the dinghy having been lowered, the oarsmen jumped in, the Bishop descended the ladder and took his seat. The men pulled at their oars and the boat moved rapidly towards the island. When they came within a stone's throw, they saw the three old hermits: a tall one with only a piece of matting tied around his waist, a shorter one in a tattered peasant coat, and a very old one bent with age and wearing a priest's cassock. All three were standing hand in hand.

The oarsmen pulled in to shore, and held on with the boathook until the Bishop got out.

The hermits bowed deeply to the Bishop, who gave them his blessing, at which they bowed still lower. Then the Bishop began to speak.

"I have heard," said he, "that you godly men live here, saving your own souls and praying to our Lord Christ for your fellow man. I, an unworthy servant of Christ, am called, by God's mercy, to keep and teach His flock. I wished to see you, servants of God, and to do what I can to teach you, also."

The old men looked at each other smiling, but remained silent.

"Tell me," said the Bishop, "what you are doing to save your souls, and how you serve God on this island."

The second hermit sighed, and looked at the oldest, the very ancient one. The latter smiled, and said:

"We do not know how to serve God. We only serve and support ourselves."

"But how do you pray to God?" asked the Bishop.

"We pray in this way," replied the hermit. "Three are ye, three are we, have mercy upon us."

And when the old man said this, all three raised their eyes to heaven, and repeated:

"Three are ye, three are we, have mercy upon us!"

The Bishop smiled.

"You have evidently heard something about the Holy Trinity," said he. "But you do not pray aright. You have won my affection, godly men. I see that you wish to please the Lord, but you do not know how to serve Him. That is not the way to pray. Listen to me, and I will teach you—not in my own way but in the way in which God in the Holy Scriptures has commanded all men to pray to Him."

Patiently, the Bishop began explaining to the hermits how God had revealed Himself to men; telling them of God the Father, and God the Son, and God the Holy Ghost.

"God the Son came down on earth," said he, "to save men, and this is how He taught us all to pray. Listen, and repeat after me: 'Our Father.'"

And the first old man repeated after him, "Our Father," and the second said, "Our Father," and the third said, "Our Father."

"Which art in heaven," continued the Bishop.

The first hermit repeated, "Which art in heaven," but the second blundered over the words, and the tall hermit could not say them properly. His hair had grown over his mouth so that he could not speak plainly. The very old hermit, having no teeth whatever, also mumbled indistinctly.

The Bishop repeated the words again, and the old men tried repeating them after him. The Bishop sat down on a stone, and the old men stood before him, watching his mouth, and saying the words as he uttered them. All day long the Bishop labored, saying a word twenty, thirty, a hundred times over, and the old men repeated it after him. They blundered, and he corrected them, and made them begin again.

The Bishop did not give up till he had taught them the whole of the Lord's Prayer so that they could not only repeat it after him, but could say it by themselves. The middle one was the first to know it, and to repeat the whole of it alone. The Bishop made him say it again and again, and at last the others could say it too.

Darkness closed in and the moon appeared over the water before the Bishop rose to return to the vessel. When he took leave of the old men, they all bowed down to the ground before him. He raised them and kissed each one, telling them to pray as he had taught them. Then he got into the dinghy, and as he was rowed back to the ship, he could hear the three voices loudly repeating the Lord's Prayer. But as he drew near the vessel, their words could no longer be heard. Yet the men could still be seen in the moonlight, standing as he had left them on the shore—the shortest in the middle, the tallest one on the right, the middle one on the left.

When the Bishop climbed aboard the big vessel, the anchor was weighed and the sails unfurled. The wind filled them and the ship sailed away. The Bishop took a seat in the stern and watched the island he had left. For a time he could still see the hermits, but presently they disappeared from sight, though the island was still visible. At last it too vanished, and only the sea remained, rippling in the moonlight.

The pilgrims lay down to sleep, and all was quiet on deck. The Bishop did not wish to sleep, but sat gazing alone at the sea, thinking how pleased the old men had been to learn the Lord's Prayer; and he thanked God for having sent him to teach and help such godly men.

Just so, the Bishop continued to muse and gaze at the sea where the island had disappeared. The moonlight flickered before his eyes, sparkling now here, now there, upon the waves. Suddenly he saw something white and shining on the bright path which the moon cast across the sea. Was it a seagull, or the little gleaming sail of some small boat? The Bishop fixed his eyes on it, wondering.

"It *must* be a boat sailing after us," he thought, "but it is overtaking us very rapidly. A moment ago it was far, far away, now it is much nearer. No, it cannot be a boat, for I can see no sail; but whatever it may be, it is following us and catching up."

Baffled, he strained his eyes to make out what it was. Not a boat, nor a bird, nor a fish! It was too large for a man, and besides, a man could not be out there in the midst of the sea. The Bishop rose, and said to the helmsman:

"Look there! What is that, my friend? *What is it?*"

Before the helmsman could answer, the Bishop saw plainly what it was—the three hermits running upon the water, all gleaming white, their grey beards shining, and approaching the ship as quickly as though it were not moving.

The steersman let go the helm in terror.

"Oh, Lord! The hermits are running after us on the water as though it were dry land!"

The passengers, hearing him, jumped up and crowded to the stern. They saw the hermits coming along hand in hand, and the two outer ones beckoning the ship to stop. All three were gliding along upon the water without moving their feet. Before the ship could be stopped, the hermits had reached it, and raising their heads, all three, as with one voice, began to say:

"We have forgotten your prayer, servant of God. As long as we kept repeating it, we remembered but when we stopped saying it for a time, a word dropped out, and now it has all gone to pieces. We can remember nothing of it. Teach us again."

The Bishop crossed himself, and leaning over the ship's side, said:

"Your own prayer will reach the Lord, men of God. It is not for me to teach you. Pray for us sinners."

And the Bishop bowed low before the old men; and they turned and went back across the sea. And a light shone until daybreak on the spot where they were lost to sight.

ROMULUS AND REMUS

The Trojan War was over, leaving in its wake the charred remains of war. The proud city of Troy had been set on fire and destroyed; most of the defenders had been slain. Only one of the leaders, Aeneas, had survived. Homeless and heartsick, Aeneas roamed about for many years. Finally, weary of his long wanderings, he settled in Italy, where he made friends, married a king's daughter, and founded a colony.

Among his descendants were two brothers, Amulius and Numitor. The older one, Numitor, became king and was a gentle ruler. But Amulius was crafty and cruel. He schemed to take over the throne. First by trickery, then by force, Amulius seized power and drove Numitor out of the royal house.

To make sure there would be no heirs to claim divine right to the throne, he put Numitor's son to death. He also wanted to do away with Numitor's daughter, Silvia, but he was afraid that the people would rise against him if he had her killed. Instead, he did what he thought was very clever: he appointed her a priestess of Vesta. Now, those who took care of the temple of Vesta were forbidden to marry. "And so," he assured himself, "there will be no children to dispute my kingship."

But Amulius' plan miscarried. Out of the forest came a man—stern and mighty of muscle, fierce but fascinating. By his side there walked a wolf, and a woodpecker sat on his shoulder. He saw Silvia and fell in love with her, and she—who shared his communion with birds and beasts—returned his love. She did not know it, but the stalwart stranger was a god in disguise, Mars, the god of war. She bore him twin sons, Romulus and Remus.

Furious at first, the wily Amulius saw how he could benefit by what had happened. Now he had a good excuse to get rid of the last threat to his throne. He had Silvia thrown into prison for breaking her vows, and he gave orders that her children should be set adrift on the Tiber River. Even in this act, Amulius was crafty. He saw to it that the babes were put into a shallow basket and floated on the roaring Tiber exactly at flood tide.

"If the basket sinks," he said, "let them swim. If they drown, it will not be my fault. The river will be to blame, not I."

The river rose higher than at any time in the memory of man. It rose so high and fast that, before the basket could sink, it was washed ashore. There, on the muddy banks of the Tiber, caught in the reeds, the infants lay shivering and crying with hunger.

Their cries were heard, not by a human being, but by a wandering animal, a she-wolf who had come down to the river to

drink. She sniffed the babies, so hairless, so homeless, so hopeless. She gave them of her milk, carried them in her mouth to her cave in the woods, and warmed them with her body. A woodpecker made its home in a nearby tree and, from time to time, brought berries to add to their survival. The god of war must have smiled.

So Romulus and Remus became part of the she-wolf's family. They played with her cubs, and shared whatever the mother brought in. As they grew older, they grew bolder, stronger, and more cunning than any of the young wolves in the wood.

One fall hunters came through the forest with dogs and daggers and surrounded the pack. But the wolf-boys were not to be caught. They slipped through the circle and found a cave of their own. There they were discovered by a shepherd, Faustulus, who was looking for stray sheep. They snarled and bared their teeth at him, but he seized them by the hair and, though they squirmed and clawed, he brought them to his home.

"Here," he said to his wife, "you always wanted children, and we haven't any. I'm not sure these two are human but, whatever they may be, they are here. Do you want to keep them or shall I turn them loose?"

She looked sharp at them and was not frightened. They looked at her and stopped snarling. Instead, they rubbed against her.

"I want to keep them," she said. "And I believe they want to stay."

For a while Romulus and Remus were little savages. They pounced upon their food and ate it whole; they slept curled up in dark corners and howled at the full moon. They were always on the heels of the shepherd's wife, following her wherever she went like a couple of faithful dogs. She was most patient, showing them, by example, how to act like human beings. She tamed them quietly and taught them with the language of love.

Gradually the boys lost their wildness. They learned to talk, they learned what to do with their hands, and how to work things out in their heads. They grew slim and tall.

As they developed into young manhood, they became expert shepherds. With an understanding of nature they had learned from the she-wolf, and the authority they had

inherited from their royal ancestors, they became the leaders of all the herdsmen far and near. There were quarrels with other groups of shepherds and fights with gangs of robbers, but the brothers were always victorious. However, one day when they were separated, a band of marauders took Remus by surprise, captured his flock of sheep, and delivered him to King Amulius for ransom.

As soon as Romulus learned what had happened, he ran to his foster-father.

"I was afraid of some happening like this," said the old shepherd. "I have been troubled about the two of you for a long time. You must realize you are not like the others."

"Who then are we?" asked Romulus.

"I'm not sure," said the shepherd, "but when you learned to talk, you told me a queer tale. You remembered that you had been cared for by a she-wolf in a shelter near the Tiber. At first this seemed impossible. Then I, too, remembered something. I remembered a rumor that King Amulius had seized the throne from his brother Numitor, that he had imprisoned Numitor's daughter, Silvia, and cast her twins into the river. You see, Romulus, I found you and your brother not far from the river and not long after the two infants were supposed to have been drowned."

Romulus stared in wonder. "You mean . . . you think Remus and I might be . . ."

"What else is there to think?" replied the shepherd. "I think—at least I guess—who you are. Also I think you might have a talk with King Amulius. Or, better still, with your grandfather Numitor. I think it's time for you to learn for certain who you are."

The next day Romulus sought out Numitor in his exile and poured out all there was to tell. The ex-monarch regarded the youth intently for a long time before he spoke.

"Yes," he said finally. "There is no question in my mind. You are of the lineage of Aeneas. You are my grandson. And your brother is the prisoner of Amulius, who tried to kill you both and who robbed me of my throne. Yet knowing all this, what can you do?"

"I can topple him from his throne," spoke Romulus.

Doubt crept into Numitor's voice. "Perhaps so," he said. "But how will you do it? Alone?"

"I can count on many friends. The shepherds will help."

"Shepherds?" Numitor lifted an eyebrow. "Shepherds for soldiers? And with what weapons?"

"Sticks, stones, clubs, shepherd's crooks—anything."

Stout-hearted though Romulus was, he knew his band was no match for the trained troops of Amulius. So at night when the shepherds, together with some of Numitor's staff, were assembled in the dark woods, Romulus devised a strategy. He gave an order to Numitor's men to dash toward the citadel that contained the treasury, rushing with fierce cries and flaming torches.

Thinking the citadel was the center of attack, the king's guards left the royal house to protect the treasury. At that moment, Romulus and his shepherds broke out of the woods, tore down the gates of Amulius' house, overpowered the remaining soldiers, and rescued Remus. Together the brothers ran through the rooms, smashed the doors of the royal private chambers, and slew the treacherous king. Again the god of war must have smiled—this time with pride.

The fight lasted less than an hour. When peace was restored, Numitor was proclaimed king and established in his rightful place. He acknowledged Romulus and Remus as princes and heroic heirs to the throne. Reunited in a joyful ceremony they swore allegiance to their royal grandfather.

But life at court was not to their liking. The pomp and ceremony seemed shallow and tiresome; they still had a love of adventure in their blood. They grew restless, wanting to create something of value, though they did not know what. Suddenly, as twins often do, they began thinking alike—of building a city, a city of their own. They even knew where it would be. They would build it on the banks of the Tiber, at the very place where they had been left to die.

Gathering their men about them, they set out to find the best place for the first foundation. They waited for a sign. Remus stood on one hill, Romulus on another. To Remus came the first sign: six vultures flying over his head. It was a good omen, for the vulture is a sacred bird, a bird that did not kill but fed only on the dead. It was the bird offered up for important sacrifices.

"We will build here," cried Remus.

But before the six vultures had soared away, another group came out of the heavens and circled above Romulus. This time there were twelve birds.

"The right place is here," shouted Romulus.

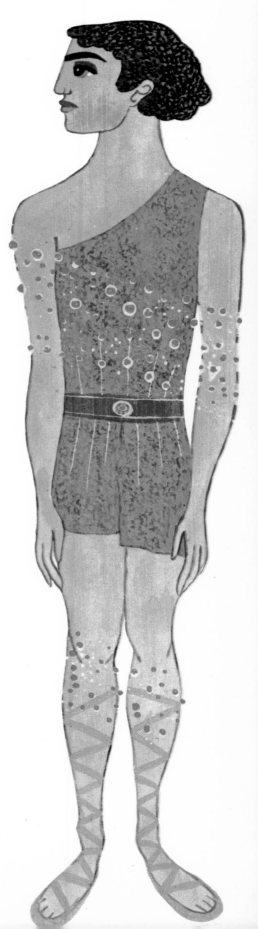

Those who stood around Remus claimed that since he had seen the birds first, the city should be built where he wished, and that Remus should be its first king. Those around Romulus insisted that since he had seen the greater number, this proved he was favored by the gods, and it was Romulus who should rule the city. Both groups argued loud and long; their voices grew angrier. The dispute led to violence and in the fighting Remus was slain.

Romulus was aghast at what had happened. He tore his clothes in anguish; he bathed the body of Remus with his tears and threatened to kill himself. But the men consoled him, blaming themselves for the tragedy. At last they succeeded in rousing him from despair. They made him realize that they had come here for a purpose, that there was work to be done, a city to be built.

Built it was, a proud city on seven hills, a city whose first king was Romulus and whose name became *Rome* in his honor. There Romulus lived and ruled and fought to preserve the city until his death. Before the end, he gathered his people about him and addressed them.

"Our city," he said, "shall one day be the greatest city in the world. Let your children teach their children the way of peace and the art of war so that no human strength can ever break the power of the Roman spirit." Then Romulus died.

They buried him in a marble sarcophagus carved with a frieze showing a basket floating on a river, a she-wolf suckling twin babies, a shepherd and his wife, and in a design around the figures were helmets and swords and spears and all the properties of the god of war. Crowning the monument they placed a vulture, the bird of sacrifice, the sacred bird that had shown Romulus the site of his city.

Years passed. The years grew into centuries; centuries piled upon each other. The dust of time sifted over the earth and into men's minds. People began to think of Romulus and Remus as legendary figures, myths rather than men.

Then one day in 1958, after more than two thousand years had gone by, workmen dug up an ancient site in the Roman Forum. It was thought to be the burial place of Romulus, though further evidence was needed to make certain. A marble coffin was found with traces of the carvings, but the strangest piece of evidence was a scattering of sacrificial bones upon the tomb. Scientists identified the bones. They were the bones of a bird, the bones of a vulture.

Mimer, the Master

At Santen, in the Lowlands, there once lived a young prince named Siegfried. His father, Siegmund, was king of the rich country, through which the lazy Rhine winds its way just before reaching the North Sea. He was known, both far and near, for his good deeds and his prudence. Siegfried's mother, the gentle Sigelind, was loved by all for her goodness of heart and her charity to the poor. Neither king nor queen left anything undone that might make the young prince happy, or fit him for life's usefulness.

Wise men were brought from far-off lands to be Siegfried's teachers; and every day something was added to his store of knowledge or his stock of happiness. Very skillful he became in warlike games and in feats of strength. No other youth could throw the spear with such great force, or shoot the arrow with surer aim. No other youth could run more swiftly, or ride with more ease. His mother took delight in adding to the beauty of his form by clothing him in garments decked with the rarest jewels.

The old, the young, the rich, the poor, the high, the low, all praised the fearless Siegfried, and all vied in friendly strife to win his favor. One would have thought that life for the young prince would be a never ending holiday, and that the birds would sing, flowers would bloom, and the sun would shine forever for his sake.

"But the business of man's life is not mere pastime; none knows this truth better than I," said the wise king, Siegmund. "All work is noble," he told Siegfried, "and he who yearns to win fame must not shun toil. Even princes should know how to earn a livelihood by the labor of their hands."

And so, while Siegfried was still a young lad, his father arranged for him to live with a smith called Mimer, whose smithy stood among the hills not far from the great forest. In those early times the work of the smith was looked upon as the worthiest of all trades—one which the gods themselves were not ashamed to follow.

Mimer was a wise master. Men said that he was akin to the dwarf-folk who had ruled the earth in the early days, and who were learned in every lore, and skilled in every craft. Mimer was so exceeding old that no one could remember the day when he came to dwell in the land of Siegmund's fathers. Some said that he was the keeper of a flowing spring, the waters of which im-

parted wisdom and far-seeing knowledge to all who drank of them.

To Mimer's school, where he would be taught to work skillfully and to think wisely, Siegfried was sent, to toil in all respects like the other pupils. A coarse blue blouse, heavy leggings, and a leathern apron took the place of the costly clothing which he had worn in his father's dwelling. His feet were encased in wooden shoes, and his head was covered with a wolfskin cap. The fine bed with its downy pillows, wherein every night his mother had been wont, with gentle care, to see him safely covered, was now traded for a rude heap of straw in a corner of the smithy. The rich food to which he was accustomed gave place to the humblest fare.

But the prince did not complain. The days which he passed in the smithy were surprisingly happy. The sound of his hammer rang cheerfully and the sparks from his forge flew like fireworks from morning till night.

In less than a year Siegfried became Mimer's prized apprentice. No one could do more work than he, and none wrought with greater skill. The heaviest chains and the strongest bolts—for prison or for treasure-house—were as toys in his stout hands, so easily and quickly did he beat them into shape. He became equally expert in work of the most delicate kind. Ornaments of gold and silver studded with gems were fashioned into jewelry by his deft fingers. Among all of Mimer's apprentices none learned the master's lore so readily, nor gained the master's favor more staunchly.

One morning Master Mimer came to the smithy with a troubled look upon his face. It was clear that something had gone amiss. What it was the apprentices soon learned from the smith himself. Until lately no one had questioned Mimer's right to be called the foremost smith in all the world. Now a rival had come forward. An unknown upstart—one Amilias of Burgundyland—had made a suit of armor which, he boasted, neither stroke of sword could dent nor blow of spear could scratch. He had sent a challenge to all other smiths, both in the Rhine country and elsewhere, to equal his piece of workmanship or acknowledge themselves his underlings.

For many days Mimer himself toiled, alone and vainly, trying to forge a sword whose edge could nick the boasted armor of

Amilias. Now, in despair, he came to ask the help of his pupils and apprentices.

"Who among you is skillful enough to forge such a sword?" he asked.

One after another the pupils shook their heads. Veliant, the foreman of the apprentices, said, "I have heard much about that wonderful armor of Amilias and its extreme hardness. I doubt if any skill can make a sword with edge so sharp and true as to cut into it. The best that can be done is to try to make another war coat whose temper shall equal that of Amilias' armor."

Siegfried then faced Veliant and Mimer. "I will make a sword such as you want—a blade that no war coat can foil. Give me but leave to try!"

The other pupils laughed in scorn, but Mimer checked them. "You hear how this boy can talk; we will now see what he can do. He is the king's son, and we know that he has uncommon talent. He shall make the sword. But if, upon trial, it fails, he shall rue the day."

Siegfried went at once to his task. For seven days and seven nights the sparks never stopped flying from his forge, and the ringing of his anvil and the hissing of the hot metal as he tempered it were heard continuously. On the eighth day the sword was fashioned, and Siegfried brought it to Mimer.

The smith felt the razor edge of the shining weapon. "This seems, indeed, a fair fire edge. Let us make a trial of its keenness."

He asked that a thread of wool as light as thistledown be thrown upon water. As it floated there, Mimer struck it with the sword. The glittering blade cleft the slender thread in twain, and the pieces floated undisturbed upon the surface of the water.

"Well done!" cried the delighted smith. "Never have I seen a keener edge. If its temper is as true as its sharpness, it will indeed serve me well."

But Siegfried took back the sword and broke it into many pieces. For three days he welded the pieces in a white-hot fire, tempering the steel with milk and oatmeal. Then, in sight of Mimer and the scornful apprentices, he cast a light ball of fine-spun wool upon the flowing water of the brook. It caught in the swift eddies and went whirling about until it met the bared blade of the new sword held in Mimer's hands. To the open-mouthed wonder of the apprentices the ball parted into halves as clean as the rippling water. Not the smallest thread was moved out of its place.

Even so, Siegfried carried the sword back again to the smithy. This time his forge glowed with a brighter fire, his hammer rang upon the anvil with a sound to reach the mountains, and he allowed none of the apprentices to come near. No one ever knew what witchery he used, but some of his fellow pupils afterwards told how, in the dusky twilight, they had seen a one-eyed stranger, long-bearded and clad in a cloud-gray kirtle with a sky-blue hood, talking with Siegfried at the smithy door. The stranger's face, they said, was at once pleasant and fearful to look upon. His one eye shone in the gloaming like the evening star, as he placed in Siegfried's hands bright shards, like pieces of a broken sword. Then he faded suddenly from their sight and was seen no more.

For seven weeks the lad wrought day and night at his forge. At last, pale and haggard, but with a pleased smile upon his face, he stood before Mimer, the gleaming sword in his hands.

"It is finished," Siegfried said. "Behold the glittering terror—the blade Balmung! Let us try its edge and prove its temper once again so we may know whether you can place your trust in it."

Mimer looked long at the ruddy hilt of the weapon and at the mystic runes scored upon its sides. He felt of the keen edge, which shimmered like a ray of sunlight in the gathering gloom of the evening. No word came from his lips; his eyes were dazed, as one lost in thoughts of days long past and gone.

Now Siegfried raised the blade high over his head, flashing the gleaming edge hither and thither, like lightning's play when Thor rides over the storm clouds. Then suddenly it fell upon the master's anvil, and the great block of iron was cleft in two, yet the blade itself was no whit dulled by the stroke, and the line of light which marked the edge was brighter than before.

Then to the flowing brook they went; and a great pack of wool, the fleece of ten sheep, was brought, and thrown upon the swirling water. As the stream bore the bundle downwards, Mimer held the sword in its way, and the bundle was divided as easily and as clean as the single woolen thread had been.

"Now indeed," cried Mimer, "I no longer fear to meet Amilias of Burgundyland. If his war coat can withstand the stroke of such a sword as Balmung, then I shall not be ashamed to be his

underling. But if this good blade is what it seems to be, it will not fail me; and I, Mimer the Old, shall still be called the wisest and greatest of smiths."

At once he sent word to Amilias in Burgundyland to meet him on a certain day and settle forever the question as to which of the two should be the master and which the underling. Heralds proclaimed the contest in every town and dwelling. When the time which had been set drew near, Mimer, bearing the sword Balmung, and followed by all his pupils and apprentices, proceeded in single file toward the place of meeting. Through the forest they went, and along the banks of the sluggish river for many a league, to the height of land which marked the line between King Siegmund's country and the country of the Burgundians.

It was in this place, midway between the shops of Mimer and Amilias, that the great trial of metal and of skill was to be made. Great numbers of people from the Lowlands and from Burgundy were already gathered, anxiously awaiting the arrival of the champions. On one side were wise King Siegmund and his gentle queen, along with their train of knights, courtiers and fair ladies. On the other side were the three Burgundian kings—Gunther, Gernot and Giselher—and a mighty retinue of warriors led by grim old Hagen, the uncle of the kings, and the wariest chief in all Rhineland.

When everything was in readiness for the contest, Amilias, clad in his war coat, climbed to the top of the hill and sat upon a great rock waiting for Mimer's coming. As he sat there, he looked to the people below like a tower of some great castle, for he was almost a giant in size. His coat of mail, skillfully wrought, was so huge that twenty men of common mould might have hidden themselves within it. As the smith Mimer, so dwarfish in stature, toiled up the steep hillside, Amilias smiled to see him; for he felt no fear of the gleaming blade that was to try the metal of his war coat. Already a shout of expectant triumph went up from the throats of the Burgundian hosts, so sure were they of their champion's success.

Mimer's friends waited in breathless silence, hoping yet fearing. Only King Siegmund whispered to his queen: "Knowledge is stronger than brute force. The smallest dwarf who has drunk from Mimer's flowing spring may safely meet the stoutest giant in battle."

When Mimer reached the top of the hill, Amilias folded his huge arms and smiled again. This contest, he felt, was mere amusement for him; Mimer was already as good as beaten.

The smith paused a moment to take breath, and as he stood by the side of his foe he seemed to those below a mere black speck beside a steel-gray tower.

"Are you ready?" asked the smith.

"Ready!" answered Amilias. "Strike!"

Mimer raised the blade in the air, and for a moment the lightning seemed to play around his head. The muscles on his short, brawny arms stood out like great ropes. Now, Balmung, descending, cleft the air from right to left. The spectators on the plain below thought to hear the noise of clashing steel but they listened in vain. No sound came to their ears, save a sharp hiss like that which red hot iron gives when plunged into a tank of cold water. The huge Amilias sat unmoved, his arms still folded upon his breast, but the smile had faded from his face.

"How do you feel now?" asked Mimer.

"Rather strangely, as if cold iron had touched me," came the faint answer.

"Shake thyself!" cried Mimer.

Amilias did so. And, lo! he fell in two halves. The sword had cut sheer through the war coat, and cleft in twain the great body encased within. Down tumbled the giant head and the still-folded arms, rolling with thundering noise to the foot of the hill where they fell with a fearful splash into the deep waters of the river. There, fathoms down, they may even now be seen when the water is clear, lying like great gray rocks among the sand and gravel below. The rest of the giant's body, with the armor which encased it, still sat upright in its place. To this day, travellers sailing down the river are shown on moonlit evenings the luckless armor of Amilias on the high hilltop. In the dim, uncertain light,

one easily fancies it to be the ivy-covered ruins of some old castle of feudal times.

With the trial over, Mimer sheathed his sword and walked slowly down the hillside to the plain, where his friends welcomed him with rousing cheers and shouts of joy. The Burgundians, baffled and vexed, turned silently homeward, not casting a single glance backward to the scene of their defeat.

Siegfried returned with the master and his fellows to the smithy, to his roaring bellows and ringing anvil, to his coarse fare, his hard bed and his life of labor. Meanwhile all men praised Mimer and his skill in forging the fiery blade. The Burgundians never knew that it was the boy Siegfried who had wrought the miracle.

In time, however, it was whispered around that not Mimer, but one of his pupils, had forged the sword. When the master was asked what truth there was in this story, his eyes twinkled, and the corners of his mouth twitched strangely. Yet he made no answer. But Veliant, the foreman of the smithy and the greatest of boasters, said, "It was I who forged the fire-edge of the blade Balmung." Although none denied his claim, few, who knew what sort of man he was, believed his story. And this is the reason that, in the ancient songs which tell of this wondrous sword, it is said by most that Mimer, and by a few that Veliant, forged its blade.

But the people of the Lowlands believe that it was made by Siegfried, the hero who afterwards wielded it in many adventures. Be this as it may, blind hate and jealousy were from this time uppermost in the selfish mind of Veliant, and he sought how he might drive the lad away from the smithy in disgrace.

"This boy has done what no one else could do," said he. "He may yet do greater deeds and set himself up as the master smith of the world, and then we shall all have to humble ourselves before him as his underlings."

Veliant nursed this thought and brooded over the hatred which he felt towards the boy; but he dared not harm him for fear of their master, Mimer. Siegfried meanwhile busied himself, and his bellows roared from early morning till late at evening. Nor did the foreman's unkindness trouble him for a moment, for he knew that the master's heart was warm towards him.

Oftentimes, when the day's work was done, Siegfried sat with Mimer by the glowing light of the furnace and listened to the tales which the master told of his deeds when the world was young, and both the dwarf-folk and the giants had a name and a place upon the earth. One night, as they sat thus, the master talked of Odin the All-Father, and of the gods who dwell with him in Asgard, and the puny menfolk whom they protect and befriend. By slow degrees his words grew full of bitterness, and his soul cried out with a fierce longing for something he dared not name. The lad's heart was stirred with a strange uneasiness, and he said,

"Tell me, I pray dear master, something about my own kin— my father's fathers—those mighty kings who were the bravest and best of men."

Then the smith seemed pleased again. His eyes lost their faraway look, and a smile played among the wrinkles of his swarthy face as he told of old King Volsung.

"Long years ago before the evil days had dawned, King Volsung ruled over all the land which lies between the sea and the country of the Goths. The days were golden with peace and plenty everywhere. Men went in and out and feared no wrong.

"Now, King Volsung had a dwelling in the midst of fertile fields and fruitful gardens. Fairer than any dream was that dwelling. The roof was thatched with gold; red turrets and towers rose above it. The great feast hall was long and high, its walls hung with sunbright shields. Even the door nails were made of pure silver. In the middle of the hall stood the pride of the Volsungs—a tree whose blossoms filled the air with fragrance, whose green branches, thrusting themselves through the ceiling, covered the roof with fair foliage. It was Odin's tree, and King Volsung had planted it there with his own hands.

"On a day in winter King Volsung held a great feast in his hall in honor of Siggeir, king of the Goths, who was his guest. Fires blazed bright in the broad chimneys, and music and laughter

went round and round. In the midst of the merrymaking the guests were startled by lightning which seemed to come from a cloudless sky and thunder which made the shields upon the walls rattle and ring. In wonder, everyone looked about until their eyes fixed on a strange man who stood smiling in the doorway, not saying a word. They noticed that he wore no shoes upon his feet, but a cloud-gray cloak encircled his body, and a blue hood was drawn down over his head. His face, half hidden by a heavy beard, had but one eye, which twinkled and glowed like a burning coal.

"The guests sat motionless in their seats, awed in the presence of him who stood at the door; for whispers went from ear to ear that he was none other than Odin the All-Father, king of gods and men. Still he spoke not, but straight into the hall he strode until he stopped beneath the blossoming branches of the tree. Then forth from beneath his cloud-gray cloak he drew a gleaming sword and struck the blade deep into the wood—so deep that nothing but the hilt was left in sight. Then turning to the guests, he said, 'A blade of mighty worth have I hidden in this tree. Never had the earth folk wrought truer steel, nor has any man ever wielded a more trusty sword. Whoever there is among you brave enough and strong enough to draw it forth from the wood, he shall have it as a gift from Odin.' Then slowly out the door he strode, and no one saw him any more.

"After he had gone, the Volsungs and their guests sat a long time in silence, fearing to stir, lest the vision should prove a dream. But at last the old king arose and cried, 'come, guests and kinsmen, set your hands to the ruddy hilt! Odin's gift waits for its fated owner. Let us see which of you is the favored of the All-Father.'

"Siggeir, king of the Goths, was first to try his hand. Then his earls, the Volsungs' guests, tried their hands. But the blade stuck fast. The stoutest man among them failed to move it. Then King Volsung, laughing, seized the hilt, and drew with all his might, but the sword held in the wood of Odin's tree.

"One by one the nine sons of Volsung tugged and strained in vain; and each was greeted with shouts of laughter as, ashamed and beaten, he wended to his seat again. Then, Sigmund, the youngest son, stood up, and laid his hand upon the ruddy hilt, scarce thinking to try what all had failed to do. When, lo! the

blade came out of the tree as if all along it had lain loose. Sigmund raised it high over his head and shook it, and the bright flame that leaped from its edge lit up the hall like a torch. The Volsungs and their guests rent the air with cheers and shouts of gladness. For no one among all the men of the mid-world was more worthy of Odin's gift than the lad, Sigmund the brave."

Mimer and his young apprentice sat for hours by the dying coals, talking of Siegfried's kinsmen and of Siggeir, the Goth king, and how he coveted Sigmund's sword and plotted to gain it by guile; and how, through pretense of friendship, he invited the Volsung kings to visit him in Gothland, and how he betrayed and slew them, save Sigmund alone, who escaped, and for long years lived as an outlaw in the land of his treacherous foe.

Then Mimer told how Sigmund afterwards came back to his own country of the Volsungs, how his people welcomed him, and he became a mighty king. Years later when Sigmund had grown old and full of years and honors, he went out with his earls and fighting men to battle against the hosts of King Lyngi the Mighty, and in the midst of the fight, when his sword had hewn down numbers of the foe and the end of the strife and victory seemed near, suddenly an old man, one-eyed, bearded, and wearing a cloud-gray cloak, stood up before him in the din. Sigmund's sword was broken in pieces, and he fell dead on the heap of the slain.

As Mimer had finished his tale, his dark face grew darker, and he cried out in a tone of despair and hopeless yearning: "Oh, past are those days of old and the worthy deeds of the brave!

These are the days of the home-stayers—of the wise, but feeble-hearted. Yet the Norns have spoken; and it must be that another hero shall arise of the Volsung blood, and he shall restore the name and the fame of his kin of the early days. And he shall be my death, for in him shall the race of heroes have an end."

Siegfried hearkened to the fateful words of the master. For a long time he sat in silent thought. Neither he nor Mimer moved or spoke again, until the darkness of night faded, and the gray light of morning stole into the smithy. Then, as if moved by a sudden impulse, Siegfried turned to the master and said.

"You speak of the Norns, dear master, and of their foretelling; but your words are vague. When shall that hero come? And who shall he be? And what deeds shall be his doing?"

"Alas!" answered Mimer, "I know not, save that he shall be of the Volsung race, and that my fate is lined with his."

"And why do you not know?" returned Siegfried. "Are you not that old Mimer, in whom it is said the garnered wisdom of the world is stored? Is there not truth in the old story that even Odin pawned one of his eyes for a single draught from your fountain of knowledge? As the possessor of so much wisdom, are you not able to look into the future with clearness and certainty?"

"Alas!" answered Mimer again, and his words came hard and slow, "I am not that Mimer, of whom old stories tell, who gave wisdom to the All-Father in exchange for an eye. He is one of the giants, and he still watches his fountain in far-off Jotunheim. I claim kinship with the dwarfs, and am sometimes known as an elf, sometimes as a wood-sprite. Men have called me Mimer because of my wisdom and skill, and the learning which I impart to my pupils. Could I but drink from the fountain of the real Mimer, then the wisdom of the world would in truth be mine, and the secrets of the future would no longer be hidden. But I must wait, as I have long waited, for the day and the deed and the doom that the Norns have foretold."

And the old strange look of longing came again to his eyes, and the wrinkles on his swarthy face deepened in agony, as he arose and left the smithy. Siegfried sat alone before the smoldering fire, and pondered upon what he had heard.

The Master Cat

There was a miller who left no more estate to the three sons he had than his mill, his donkey, and his cat. The division was soon made. Neither scribe nor attorney was sent for; they would soon have eaten up all the poor inheritance. The eldest received the mill, the second the donkey, and the youngest nothing but the cat. The poor young lad was quite comfortless at having so meager a lot.

"My brothers," said he, "may get their living handsomely enough by joining their stocks together. But for my part, when I have eaten my cat, and made me a muff of his skin, I must die of hunger."

The cat, who heard all this, said to his master with a very grave and serious air, "Do not thus afflict yourself, sir. You need only give me a bag, and have a pair of boots made for me that I may scamper through the brambles. You shall see you have not so poor a portion with me as you imagine."

The cat's master had often seen him play a cunning trick to catch rats and mice; he would hide himself in a sack of grain and play dead. "Perhaps," the youngest son said to himself, "I should not altogether despair."

When the cat was given what he had asked for, he booted himself very gallantly, and putting his bag about his neck, he held the strings of it in his forepaws and dived into a warren where lived a great abundance of rabbits. Beforehand he had stuffed bran and lettuce into his bag. Now, stretching out at length as if dead, he waited for some young rabbits—not yet acquainted with the deceits of the world—to come and rummage for the tasty food in his bag.

Scarce had he lain down when the excitement began: a rash and foolish young rabbit jumped into the bag. Instantly, Monsieur Puss pulled the strings and killed him without pity. Proud of his prey, he pranced with it to the palace, and asked to speak with his majesty. He was shown into the king's apartment, and, making a low reverence, said to him:

"I have brought you, sir, a rabbit from the warren of my noble master, the Marquis of Carabas." (That was the grand title Puss was pleased to give his master.) "He has commanded me to present it to your Majesty from him."

"Tell your master," said the king, "that I thank him, and that he gives me a great pleasure."

The next day the cat hid himself among some standing corn. He held his bag open, and after a slight wait a brace of partridges ran into it. Quickly he drew the strings and caught them both. Again, with a bow and a flourish, he made a present of these to the king as he had the rabbit. The king, in like manner, received the partridges with great pleasure, and ordered some silver coins to be given the cat.

Thus, for two or three months, Monsieur Puss continued to carry to his majesty delicate game for his table.

One day when he knew for certain that the king was to take the air along the riverside with his daughter—the most beautiful princess in all the world—he said to his master:

"If you will follow my advice carefully, your fortune is made. You have nothing to do but wash yourself in the river, at a point I shall show you, and leave the rest to me."

The Marquis of Carabas did what the cat advised him to do, without knowing why or wherefore. While he was washing, the cat slyly hid his master's clothes under a rock, then ran to the road just in time to meet the king's carriage.

"Help! Help!" he shrilled. "My Lord Marquis of Carabas is going to be drowned."

At this the king put his head out of the coach window, and finding it was the cat who had often brought him such good game, he commanded his guards to run immediately to the rescue of his lordship, the Marquis of Carabas. While they were drawing him out of the river, the cat came up to the coach and told the king that while his master was washing, there came by some rogues who made off with his clothes, though he had cried out, "Thieves! Thieves!" several times, as loud as he could.

The king at once commanded his guards to run to the officers of his wardrobe and fetch one of his best suits for the Marquis of Carabas.

The fine clothes they brought might have enhanced any wearer, but the miller's son was tall, sturdy, and very handsome in his person. He now seemed more prince than pauper. The king's daughter took a secret inclination to him, and the Marquis of Carabas had no sooner cast two or three respectful and tender glances upon her than she fell in love with him to distraction.

The king graciously invited the Marquis to step into the coach and take the air with them. The cat, quite overjoyed to see his project begin to succeed, marched on ahead. Meeting with some countrymen, who were mowing a meadow, he said to them:

"Good people, you who are mowing, if you do not tell the king that the meadow you mow belongs to my Lord Marquis of Carabas, you shall be chopped as small as herbs for the pot."

The king did not fail to ask the mowers to whom the meadow belonged.

"To my Lord Marquis of Carabas," they answered all together, for the cat's threat had made them terribly afraid.

"You see, sir," said the marquis, "this is a meadow which never fails to yield a plentiful harvest every year."

Master Cat, who still went on before, met next with some reapers, and said to them, "Good people, you who are reaping, if you do not tell the king that all this corn belongs to my Lord Marquis of Carabas, you shall be chopped as small as herbs for the pot."

The king, who passed by a moment after, wished to know to whom all that corn belonged.

"To my Lord Marquis of Carabas," replied the reapers. The king was pleased with the answer, as well as with the marquis, whom he congratulated thereupon.

The cat, who went always before, made the same threat to all he met, and the king was astonished at the vast estates of the Marquis of Carabas.

At last Monsieur Puss came to a stately castle, the owner of which was an ogre, the richest ever known. All the lands which the king had passed belonged to this ogre. With his usual cunning, the cat had taken care to inform himself who this ogre was and what he could do. Asking to speak with him, he said in his most purring manner, "I could not possibly travel so near your castle without paying my respects."

The ogre received him as civilly as an ogre could, and bade him sit down.

"I have been assured," said the cat, "that you have the gift of transforming yourself into any sort of creature whatever. You can, for example, change yourself into a lion or elephant and the like."

"That is true," answered the ogre briskly, "and to convince you, you shall see me now become a lion."

Puss was so badly terrified at the sight of a lion stalking him that he immediately got into the rain gutter, not without abundance of trouble and danger because of his boots, which were made for running.

Minutes later, when the ogre resumed his natural form, Puss admitted he had been much frightened. Speaking very coolly now, he said, "I have been moreover informed—yet I know not how to believe it—that you have also the power to change yourself into the shape of the smallest animal; for example, into a rat or a mouse. But I must own to you I take this to be impossible."

"Impossible!" cried the ogre. "You shall see!" Instantly he changed himself into a mouse and began to scurry about the floor. Puss no sooner perceived this than he fell upon him and ate him up.

By now the king was approaching the fine castle of the ogre, and had a mind to go into it. Puss, who heard the noise of his majesty's coach clattering over the drawbridge, ran out, announcing to the king:

"Welcome, your Majesty, to the castle of my Lord Marquis of Carabas."

"What, my Lord Marquis!" cried the king. "And does this castle also belong to you? There can be nothing finer than this court and all the stately buildings which surround it. Let us go in, if you please."

The marquis gave his hand to the princess and followed the king, who went first. They passed into a spacious hall, where they found a magnificent collation, which the ogre had prepared for his friends, who were at that moment coming to visit him; but the friends dared not enter, knowing the king was there.

His majesty was utterly charmed with the qualities of the Lord Marquis of Carabas—as was his daughter. Noting the vastness of the estate, the king said to him:

"It will be owing to yourself only, my Lord Marquis, if you are not my son-in-law."

The marquis, making several low bows, accepted the honor which his majesty conferred upon him, and forthwith, that very same day, married the princess.

Master Cat became a great lord, and never deigned to run after mice and rats any more.

David and Goliath

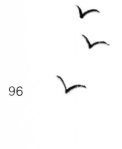

Of all Bible stories, one of the most dramatic is the tale of David, the shepherd boy, and his encounter with the champion warrior of the Philistines.

David was the youngest son of a farmer. His older brothers had gone off to be soldiers in the Israelite army. David was left to tend the sheep and goats that grazed on his father's pastures. He was a handsome youth, almost godly to look upon.

Besides being a shepherd, David was a music-maker. When King Saul was threatened by the Philistines and troubled by worrisome thoughts, one of his servants sent for the boy David to play before the king. David brought his harp and swept the chords with such harmony that he brought consolation to Saul. The king was pleased with the boy and made David his armor-bearer.

But Saul was constantly harassed by the enemy who now declared war on Israel. The time for a final decision had come. The Philistines and the Israelites faced each other on opposite mountains.

The leader of the Philistines was Goliath of Gath, a giant ten feet high. He was a frightening figure not only because of his brute strength but also because of his mighty armor. He wore a helmet of heavy brass, a coat of steel mesh, plates of reinforced metal on his legs, and he carried an iron spear that weighed twenty pounds.

Goliath stepped out from the Philistine ranks, and stood before the Israelites, taunting:

"You are a puny lot to think of battling. Choose a man and let him come to me. If he be able to fight and kill me, then the Philistines will be your servants. But if I prevail and kill him, then shall you serve us."

When Saul heard these words, he and all Israel were dismayed and knew not what to do.

Meanwhile David had returned to the farm to help his aged father. One day the father called his youngest son to him and said, "Take this basket of food to your soldier brothers—it holds bread and cheese and other provisions—and tell me how they fare."

David arrived just as Goliath shouted his mocking challenge. He had jeered at the Israelites many times, but no one had answered. David was shocked. "Why are you afraid?" he asked of the men about him. "Goliath may be big, but he is only a man. I will fight him."

When King Saul heard of this, he argued with David. "You are brave, but you are only a shepherd boy. This Philistine has been a man of war from his youth."

"Once when I was taking care of the sheep," said David, "there came a lion, and he took a lamb from the flock. I went after him and seized the lion by his hair; I grappled with him, slew the lion, and saved the lamb. If I could face a lion, surely I should not fear a Philistine who dares defy the army of the Lord."

Saul put his hand on David's shoulder. "You are resolute," he said. "I will not stop you. Go, and the Lord go with you."

David was about to leave, but Saul motioned him to stay. "Let me arm you properly," he said. "At least you should be as well equipped as the giant."

He put his own helmet on David's head, girded him with his own coat of mail, and placed his own sword in his hand.

David thanked him, but as soon as he was outside, he removed the armor to which he was not accustomed and which only hampered him. He took his shepherd's crook, a thing he knew how to use, and looked for something else with which he was familiar. He picked five smooth stones from a brook, put them in his shepherd's bag, and tested his sling. Then he called to Goliath. "Where is the braggart of Gath?"

Goliath came forth, saw the unarmed boy with nothing but a shepherd's crook, and sneered. "Do you think I am a dog that you come at me with a stick?"

When David did not answer, Goliath grew furious. "Come a little nearer and I will give

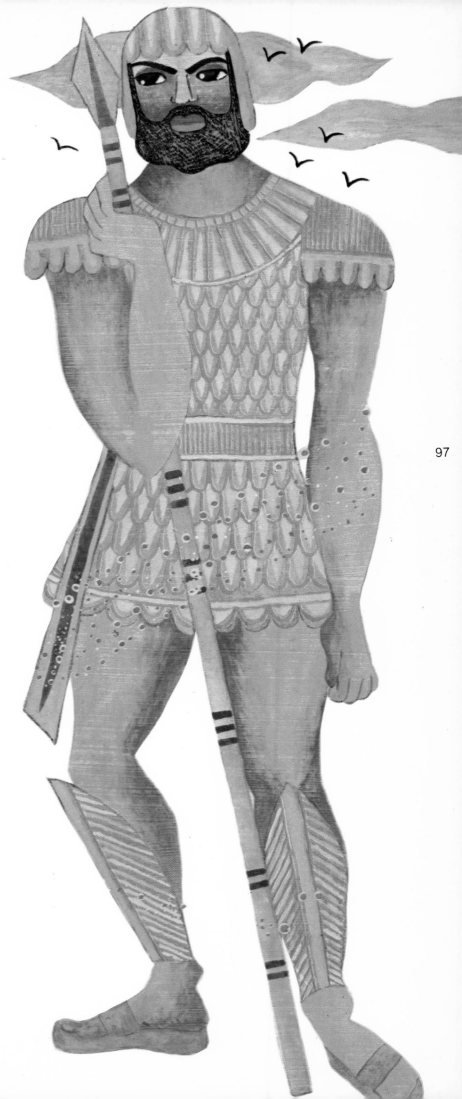

your flesh to the fowls of the air and to the beasts of the field!"

David replied, "You come with a sword and a spear. But I come in the name of the Lord of hosts, the God of the army of Israel. The Lord will deliver you into my hand, and it will be your flesh, not mine, that will feed the fowls of the air and the beasts of the field. And all the earth will know that there is a God in Israel."

Goliath took a giant's step forward. As he advanced, David slid his hand in his shepherd's bag and took out a smooth stone. He fitted it into the sling, and taking careful aim, hurled the stone at the oncoming giant. It hit the Philistine and sank deep into his forehead. With a mighty clank of armor, Goliath fell dead.

The Israelites shouted with joy. "His head! His head!" they cried. David sprang forward, and since he had no sword of his own, he drew Goliath's sword from its sheath, and cut off the giant's head.

When the Philistines saw that their champion had been killed by an unarmed boy, they cowered at the miracle, threw down their arms and fled. And Israel was once more at peace.

Rama

Prince Rama of India had been brought up in the court of his father, King Dasaratha. By the time he was sixteen he was more mature than most men. His body had been hardened by countless exercises and preparations for manhood. He was expert in wrestling, running, horsemanship, and swordsmanship. His mind had been developed by studies in philosophy, mathematics, and music. He was ready for whatever life had to offer.

One day an elderly sage entered the court and was given an audience with the king.

"I, too, was once a king," said the sage. "But I gave up the throne for a better way of life. It is for the less worldly life that I make a request."

"As one who is still worldly, I listen," Dasaratha replied. "Name your request, and I shall try to grant it."

"Let me have your son, Rama, for a while," said the sage. "He seems prepared for any adventure. He is strong in body and sound in mind. But he knows little of the spirit. Let me show him the power of meditation and the power of prayer."

Dasaratha hesitated. "You ask me to give you the joy of my middle years and the hope of my old age. It is asking a great deal."

"I ask not only for Rama's sake but also for the sake of the people," said the sage. "Our village has been ruined by a supernatural monster which is spreading terror through the rest of the country. Only one who combines physical prowess with spiritual strength can defeat it. That is why I ask for Rama."

Before Dasaratha could reply, Rama spoke up. "Father, let me go. I would gladly learn what I lack. Even more gladly would I rid the country of the monster. I beseech you, let me go."

"Who could deny you your right to learn?" said Dasaratha. "Nor would I hinder you from employing all your powers, especially in a good cause. So be it. You may go."

The way to the sage's village was seemingly endless. It took weeks and months of travel. On the long journey Rama was instructed in prayers, chants, and meditations.

One early morning the sage said: "Your soul, Rama, is now as pure as your body is perfect. You are religion itself. Now you are ready for whatever may befall."

As if to challenge those words, the air thundered with an earth-quaking roar. A huge elephant-like creature with tusks like

ten-foot spears and a head like a burning furnace charged upon them. Rama sped arrow after arrow at the monster's throat. Though he wounded it, the beast continued to thrust at them with its death-dealing tusks. Rama uttered a prayer for survival

and shot his last arrow. It tore through the air, a fearful shaft of lightning, and lodged in the monster's heart. Black smoke curled from its mouth like a horde of writhing serpents, and its death cry shattered the trees.

"Evil cannot touch you," said the sage. "Now let us see if your strength of purpose is great enough to bend the bow that has never been bent."

"What bow is that?" inquired Rama.

"In the city of Mithila lives the flowerlike Sita, daughter of King Janaka. Ever since her fifteenth year, princes have come from all over India to woo her. Her father has forbidden anyone to court her who cannot bend the bow of everlasting power—the bow which cannot be bent."

"I would like to see that bow which cannot be bent," said Rama. "And I would also like to look upon the lovely Sita. Let us go to Mithila."

After four days' journeying, they reached the capital at night. It was a brilliant city, blazing with lights of every color. Royal banners snapped in the air, bursts of music greeted the visitors. Rama could scarce wait for what the morning would bring.

As a king's son, Rama was used to luxury. But when he stood before King Janaka in the high vaulted throne-room with walls of marble set with rubies, sapphires, and emeralds, he knew that he had never seen anything as magnificent. Then, looking at Sita, who sat next to her father, he knew he had never seen any maiden as desirable. She returned his gaze and smiled. He had never seen her before, yet he seemed to recognize her. Perhaps she was some divinity he had worshiped in a dream. Perhaps he had known her in some other life. Perhaps, in that other life, he had been her lover. But it was this life that Rama was now thinking about. He caught his breath in excitement as a herald announced that the ceremonies were about to begin.

First there was music: flute-playing punctuated by the light clashing of cymbals, the low-droning tambourine, and singing accompanied by the sitar, a magically stringed guitar named in honor of the princess. Then there was solemn dancing, the performers weaving to and fro like plumed birds following some slow, half-forgotten ritual. Then came the hour of meditation. At last six servants brought in the bow.

"As you see," said King Janaka, "it takes six men to carry the bow. It is difficult enough to lift, and has never been bent. There is a prophecy that it can be lifted only by the bravest, but only the purest as well as the strongest can bend it. Does anyone care to attempt the trial?"

The bow was placed on velvet cushions on the floor. The first contestant, a young noble with jewels in his turban, came forward. He took hold of the bow, but try as he might, it would not be budged. A second youth, a tall prince from Hindustan, grasped the bow, strained to raise it an inch, and fell in exhaustion. A third, a fourth, and a fifth failed equally. The remaining contestants drew back in shame, their eyes fixed on the bow as if it were a deadly python.

Sita had shown no interest in the proceedings. Now she looked at Rama. He moved toward the velvet cushions, bowed to the king, and bowed even more deeply to Sita. He clasped his hands, bent his head, and uttered a silent prayer. Then he leaned over, put his hands on the bow and slowly lifted it to his ankles, then to his chest, and then very slowly, but without exerting himself, he lifted it above his head. The murmur that ran through the room was a mixture of admiration and astonishment. The murmur grew to uncontrollable shouting as Rama took the two ends of the bow and bent it until the ends touched. Now, placing the bow across his knee, he snapped it in half as though it were a slender reed. The shouting threatened to crack the marble walls.

There was total silence as the king left his throne to place a crown on Rama's head. And when Rama looked at Sita, her lips formed the syllables, "Rama, Rama," and she crossed her small flowerlike hands over her heart and bowed as the loving wife, waiting to serve her lord.

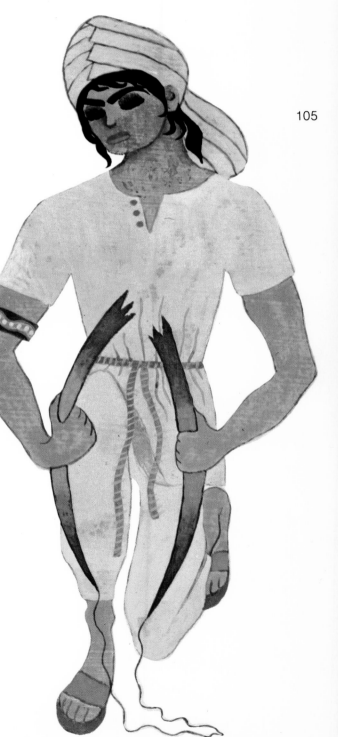

The Black Charger

Don Hernando was a brave knight who had spent all his life in the service of Spain. He had nothing to call his own but his stout armor, his fiery black charger, and his lance. With these he was in the thickest of the fray against the Moors. But one day his luck failed, and the Moors contrived to surround him and inflict grave wounds.

When his faithful black charger felt the body of his master go limp, he turned and bore him out of the fight to a lonely dell where a hermit had oft befriended them.

A grasping Moor, seeing the helpless man thus borne along, determined to possess himself of Don Hernando's armor and his bold, black steed. He galloped in pursuit, but his attempts to catch the horse were fruitless until the animal pleased to stop before the hermit's cave. There it waited patiently while they lifted his master down—the hermit and the Moor together. When the dying breath had left Don Hernando's body, the Moor stripped him of his armor and packed it carefully on the back of the charger. Being afraid to mount him, he prepared to lead him home.

But no sooner was his dead master safely in the care of the hermit and the armor safe in his own care, than the black charger dashed off at his greatest speed, leaving the Moor who had dared lay hands on his reins to measure his length in the dust. On and on the horse fled, not stopping for rest till he reached Hernando's hillside home.

Doña Teresa, Hernando's wife, had never ceased to hope and pray for her husband's return. When she saw the black charger with the armor on his back, she knew at once what had happened. Griefstricken, she took the precious armor and laid it safely away. Then she caressed the faithful animal and led him to a comfortable stall.

In the days that followed she tried the armor on her son, who was also named Hernando. She made him mount the great charger and perform feats of strength so that he, like his father, might be valiant against the Moors. But young Hernando was slight and pallid. He shrank from the hard, cold armor, and from the fiery steed. But his mother, brave as became the wife of a valiant knight, would not listen to his fears. She begged him to be of good spirit and inspired him with her courage.

At last the day came when she sent him forth to battle against the Moors. Young Hernando's heart beat high for he yearned to add his name to the traditions of prowess and valor of his father's house.

Being young, however, and untried, he shrank from the thought of pain, but he could not deny his mother's wish; so he mounted the black charger.

The animal pranced and snorted in eagerness to reach the battle ground and rout the enemy. On the way they travelled by night and slept in the heat of the day.

One early morning as they crossed a plain, young Hernando spied a tall Moor coming toward them. His heart raced in fear. Gladly would he have turned out of the way, but there was no choice. He willed his hands to be steady on the reins. A Christian, he thought, cannot shrink before a Moor. So he summoned all his courage and rode onward.

Now, when the wind brought the scent of the Moor to the bold black charger, he shook his mane and dashed forward to the encounter. Young Hernando was borne along, and found himself face to face with his foe.

In a miracle his father's shield rose to protect him and the lance lifted up his arm. Straight rode the black charger and the lance cast the Moor from his seat. Then the sword leaped from the scabbard, and fixing itself in young Hernando's grasp, struck off the pagan's head.

Hernando tied the head to his saddle and found the body still upon the Moor's mule. Thus he rode on to the royal town of Burgos. When the people saw him astride the black charger, and the headless body following along on the African mule, they cried:

"All hail to the victor! All hail to young Hernando, who conquered the pagan Moor!"

They brought him to the King, with the headless rider behind. The King rose from his throne and embraced him, and the Queen gave him her fair hand to kiss.

"A youth so comely and valiant," she said, "should have armor rich and bright and a young steed with a shining coat."

She called a page to bring a suit of polished steel and a splendid horse from the royal stables and presented both to young Hernando. Royal attendants took off his worn armor and

laid it on the back of the old black charger. And Hernando donned the new, bright suit and mounted the royal horse.

The old black charger pawed the earth and snorted to be thus set aside. Turning his head, he slow-footed his way back to Doña Teresa. When she heard his slow hoofbeats and saw him bearing the empty armor, she was certain that her son had been killed by the Moors. Again she took the precious armor and laid it safely away. Then she caressed the faithful horse and led him to his comfortable stall.

Young Hernando, meanwhile, was in a state of panic as he sat on the skittish steed the Queen had given him. He was used to the faithful, black charger of his father's. This gift of the Queen's was untried. Nor had Hernando learned to handle the new weapons. But the King, who had seen him come in from successful combat, took him for a practical warrior and gave him such work as needed a valiant heart. He sent him at once to guard the road.

"Now keep the pass open," he said, "for the rocks are narrow and high. One at a time, as the enemy comes, you will strike them down with your shining new sword."

Young Hernando's spirit was bold, though his flesh shrank. As he watched alone at the pass, with only the moon for a guide, he cried:

"Oh, had I only my old black steed, and my father's tried and trusty armor!"

In his far-off stall, the bold black charger sensed that his master's son was in danger. He trumpeted to the heavens and reared and tugged to get away. When Doña Teresa heard the noise, she knew that somewhere there was dire need for him. Quickly she bound the armor on his back, and away he fled like the wind, nor stopped till he reached Hernando.

"To me! My faithful, black steed! To me! 'Tis yet in time!" And Hernando clad himself in his father's armor and mounted the bold charger.

Stealthily in the night came the Moors, creeping through the pass. And one by one they were laid low on the ground by Hernando's lance and Hernando's sword.

When the King came the next morning, and saw that Hernando was at his post and his foes lay fallen around him, he was greatly pleased.

"You have acquitted yourself most bravely," he said. "I shall give you another suit of armor and a new bright-coated steed."

"Good King!" Hernando replied. "Pray leave me my father's armor and my father's faithful charger. I am but a stripling and my muscles are weak. It is my father's arms and my father's steed alone that have put the foe to flight."

The King let him have his will, and immediately sent him on a second mission—to carry a message of encouragement to the besieged Don Diaz whom the Moors were harassing.

With the black charger flying, the message was delivered within the hour and Hernando was again on his way, carrying a message back to the King. Suddenly, in crossing a plain, he sighted wave upon wave of Moorish horsemen arrayed in all their might.

The message to the King! He must not endanger it by encountering so overpowering a host.

It was in vain that he tried to turn, for the bold black steed refused. As if he had been cruelly spurred, he dashed right into the pagan midst. The lance sprang into Hernando's hand and pierced through the heart of the Moorish king. Then the host, dismayed, cried out:

"One rider, alone in his strength, is no mortal man. He is one of the Christian saints come down to scatter the Prophet's band."

So they turned and fled, but the black charger followed close behind, and Hernando's lance and Hernando's sword laid low the straggling host.

By day's end such fear had fallen on all the Prophet's children that on bended knee they begged for truce. They agreed to set free all their captives, and with tribute and with hostages made peace with the Christian King.

In triumph and in peace young Hernando rode home—to his home on the steep hillside. Doña Teresa came out to greet her son and his brave mount. With her walked fair Melisenda, who gave Hernando gentle greeting. She became his betrothed, and now that peace was made, they could live in love and happiness in their hillside home.

Doña Teresa stroked the bold black charger and led him to his freshly littered stall.

It is said that while the land held the blight of one pagan Moor or when a siege threatened and the Christian host needed aid, the black charger bore his master to turn the tide.

Where the steed died or when he fell, the world never knew.

Painted Skin

Once in a large city in China, a certain Mr. Wang was out walking along a road one day, when he saw a pretty young lady who was carrying a bundle and trying to make as much haste as she could. She couldn't walk very fast because in those days the feet of little girls of good birth were all cramped and bound so that when they were grown, their feet were very small and not much good for walking.

This young lady didn't seem to know her way, so Mr. Wang asked if he could be of any use. Since she seemed to be barely sixteen, he was surprised to see her out by herself, for this was not at all the proper thing in China in those days.

"I'm very much afraid you can't help me," she answered. "The fact is that I have run away from my master and mistress, and have no home to go to, nor any friend who would take me in."

"No home?" Mr. Wang asked.

"My parents," she explained, "sold me when I was quite young. They have spent the money, and if I went back to them they would certainly return me to my cruel master and mistress."

Mr. Wang felt so sorry for her that he invited her to come and hide in his house, and as he was afraid that the servants or his wife might let out where she was, he hid her in his own library, which was in a sort of garden-room separate from the rest of the house. Nobody went in and out but himself. There she stayed hidden, and Mr. Wang himself brought her food.

After a few days, when he thought it would be safe to do so, Mr. Wang told his wife about the young lady. Mrs. Wang didn't like the idea of keeping her at all.

"Because," said she, "this girl probably belongs to people in a very rich and great family. We may get into trouble, dear husband, if they find out she is here."

But Mr. Wang only smiled and shook his head. He said, "Dear wife, you are being far too nervous. I believe we can quite safely shelter the poor runaway a little longer."

Soon afterward, however, when Mr. Wang was again walking quietly along the road, he met a priest whom he knew, who looked at him very hard indeed.

"What strangers have you met lately?" asked the priest sharply.

"Oh, I don't know! No one in particular!" answered Mr. Wang. "What do you mean?"

"What I mean," answered the priest, "is that you are in the power of a witch. How can you tell me that you have met 'no one in particular'?" With that the priest stalked away, not listening to Mr. Wang's answer, but only muttering to himself, "What a fool! What a fool! He doesn't know how close he is to dying."

Mr. Wang overheard the priest and felt frightened indeed. As he walked home again, he began to think of the stranger hidden away in his library. Yet it seemed absurd to imagine that such a pretty young girl could be a witch and could want to harm him. When he arrived at his house, he thought he would go to the library and have a look. But when he tried to open the outside door, he found it bolted; so he had to climb over a wall to get to the inside door. This too he found shut and bolted.

However, his library window was close by, and he crept very softly up to it and looked through.

There, in full sight, was a hideous witch with a green face and teeth as jagged as a saw. The witch had spread a girl's skin upon the bed that had been put into the library for her, and she was painting away at this skin with a fine paintbrush. When it was finished to her liking, she threw the paintbrush into a corner, took up the skin, gave it a shake, and put it on. In a moment, what Mr. Wang saw seemed to be a graceful, modest young girl.

Mr. Wang climbed back over the wall and ran into town as fast as his shaking legs would carry him. He ran here and he ran there, searching the town from end to end, until he found the priest who had warned him.

"Save me! Save me!" he cried, throwing himself upon his knees before the priest. Then he told all he had seen.

The priest shook his head gravely. "I'm afraid," he said to Mr. Wang, "that things have gone so far I can be of little help.

"However," he added, "I can at least give you this fly-whisk. Hang it outside your bedroom door and then, later, come and meet me at the temple."

So Mr. Wang went home with the fly-whisk—the sort that they make out of a yak's tail. He didn't go near the library, but carefully hung up the whisk outside his bedroom. Then he called

to his wife and they both went into the room and shut the door. In a trembling voice, Mr. Wang told the whole story. He had scarcely finished when they heard footsteps outside.

"Peep out!" Mr. Wang whispered to his wife; he was lying on the bed by now and looking very ill. Mrs. Wang peeped out and saw the girl standing outside the door looking at the fly-whisk as though she were afraid of it. She wasn't pretty at all, but was frowning and grinding her teeth as if she were in a rage. To Mrs. Wang's relief, she went away after a moment but then, almost directly, back she came. This time she was stamping and crying out as if she were quarrelling with some unseen person.

"Don't think I'm frightened of you, Priest! Mr. Wang belongs to me, and I won't give him up!"

Then Mrs. Wang saw that the girl was tearing the whisk to pieces. When it was gone, the girl crashed open the door and walked in.

She said not a word but marched straight up to the bed on which Mr. Wang was lying, ripped open his body and tore out his heart. Then off she went with it, taking no notice of Mrs. Wang, who, ever since the witch had marched in, had been screaming at the top of her voice.

The servants heard her and now ran to see what was the matter. What they found was Mr. Wang lying dead, with a most horrible gash in his body, and Mrs. Wang screaming and trembling with fright.

"Fetch your master's brother!" she said, as soon as she could speak. Luckily Mr. Wang's brother and his wife lived only next door, so he was soon with her.

Meantime Mrs. Wang had got her wits, and now she begged her brother-in-law to go off at once to the temple to meet the priest, who was expecting her husband.

The brother went in great haste and told the priest what had happened. The priest was furious, for what was plain to him was that the witch had got the better of him. So he accompanied the brother to Mr. Wang's house. When they got there, they found only Mrs. Wang, the dead body, and the weeping servants. The witch had disappeared, and no one knew where.

The priest looked around and about. "She's still quite close," he concluded. "She must be in those rooms over there," and he pointed toward the house of Mr. Wang's brother.

"No, no, surely not!" cried Wang's brother in a terrible fright.

He and the priest ran next door and asked of this Mrs. Wang if she had seen a beautiful young girl. She said, "No, but only a little while ago a nice clean old woman came to me and offered to be our maid-of-all-work. I engaged her on the spot!"

"That old woman is the witch," cried the priest. He dashed outside and stood on guard with a wooden sword in his hand.

"O evil witch, give me back my fly-whisk!" he shouted.

When she heard the priest's voice, the nice-looking old woman came out of the house and made a break to escape. She tried to run past the priest, but he hit her with his wooden sword and down she fell in a heap. At that, the old-woman disguise dropped off her, and then the pretty-girl disguise, and there on the ground lay a hideous witch, grunting like a pig. The priest took his wooden sword and chopped off her head, but at once she turned into a thick column of smoke which seemed to curl up from the ground. And still that wasn't the end of her! The priest knew what next to do. Into the middle of the smoke he threw an uncorked gourd. Those who were watching heard a curious noise, and saw that the column of smoke was being sucked into the gourd. The priest quickly corked it. Then he rolled up the painted skins and was quietly walking away when the widowed Mrs. Wang rushed forward and threw herself on the ground at his feet, crying:

"Don't leave us! Please, please help bring back my husband to life!"

The priest shook his head. "I can't make a dead man come to life, I'm sorry to say. But I know someone who can. Only he must be asked properly."

Through her tears and sobs, Mrs. Wang said she was ready to do anything and ask anyone—properly.

"Very well," said the priest, "then I'll tell you. Down in the dirtiest part of the town, there lives a madman. He spends all his time rolling about in the mud. You must go to him, kneel in the dirt before him, and beg him to help you. You dare not take offence however rude he is to you, however he prods you. Above all things, don't lose your temper!" With these words and no more the priest went out of the gate and was soon out of sight.

Mrs. Wang braved her fears and hurried off as fast as she could. She soon came to a part of the town where she had never been before—very smelly and dirty it was, all narrow streets of hovels with rubbish-heaps in front of the doors. She found the madman quite easily. He was even more filthy and disgusting than she had imagined, but she knelt down before him as she had been told and begged him to help her. Instead of listening, he shouted all manner of rude and wicked things, and went on at the poor woman until his bellowing brought a crowd of people to see what was happening.

They saw the madman standing over Mrs. Wang, beating her with his stick, while she, poor thing, still knelt there and made no sound. At last he grew bored trying to make her angry, so he gave her a perfectly loathsome dose of medicine, and in a disagreeable voice told her to gulp it and be off. The stuff was very hard to swallow, but she managed it somehow and now the madman, with a nasty last word, walked into an old half-ruined temple close by, leaving Mrs. Wang alone with the crowd.

Poor Mrs. Wang felt only too sure that all her good temper and endurance had been useless. She ran home, feeling so ashamed of what the crowd had seen her put up with that she wished she also were dead. However, Mr. Wang's body must now be tidied up and got ready for the funeral. As the servants

were too frightened to go into the bedroom, she went in and for a beginning tried to mop up the blood and close up the terrible gash in his body.

While she worked she wept, and her sobs were so deep that they shook her whole body and seemed to bring a lump right up into her throat. Not only into her throat but into her mouth, then out of her mouth.

Pop! Something fell right into Mr. Wang's wound.

As she stooped, she saw that what had fallen was a human heart, and in another moment it began to throb in Mr. Wang's body as though it were coming to life. Trembling in awe, she closed the flesh and the skin over the heart, and then bound the wound up as tightly as she could. She heaped the bedclothes over her husband, and began briskly rubbing his hands to get them warm. By and by she heard a gentle breathing, and before long, to her joyous amazement, Mr. Wang opened his eyes, and he was indeed alive again.

In a few days he was as well as ever, except for a very slight pain in his heart and for a tiny scar where the rightful wound had been. In a few months even the scar disappeared.

121

Pecos Bill Meets Paul Bunyan

Even though Pecos Bill was boss of all the cowhands on the ranch, and had the very finest horse in all the world to ride, and had invented roping and many new skills, he was not satisfied. He wanted to start a new ranch. A small place of just a few hundred thousand acres would do to begin with, he thought.

Whenever he had a little time to spare, he rode out on Lightning (his horse), looking for a good place to start a ranch. In those days there was plenty of acreage that anyone could own simply by claiming it. But Pecos Bill did not want just an ordinary ranch. He wanted the best ranch in all the world.

Finally in Arizona he found the very piece of land that he was looking for: grass taller than a man's head for the cattle to fatten on, creeks fed by springs of pure water for them to drink, and a few trees along the banks of the creeks for shade in the heat of the day. The land was level, except for one mountain—heavily wooded almost to its peak. Strange birds, seen nowhere else in the world, built their nests among the rocks on the upper slopes. They all laid square-shaped eggs, because round eggs would have rolled right down the mountain.

Pecos Bill thought that this land with its lone mountain would be just right for his headquarters ranch. The cattle could always roam up or down to find the climate they liked best. On cold days they could graze at the foot of the mountain; in hot weather they could move up near the top, where it would always be cool. They could even have sunshine or shade, just as they wished, for one side of the mountain would be sun-bathed while the other would be shaded. Nor would there be rain on both sides at once; the cattle could almost always keep dry unless they preferred to be rain-washed. Certainly, the wind could not blow from more than one direction at once, so the herds could always find a sheltered place.

There was just one thing wrong with the mountain. It was covered with trees, huge trees, clear up to the rocky rim. There was not room to ride a horse through the close-set trees, and certainly no room for cattle to graze there.

Pecos Bill thought and thought, but he was baffled. How could he clear the mountain of those trees? He hated to give up and admit there was anything that he could not do. Again and again he rode back to look at the mountain, trying to figure out some way to clear it for his headquarters ranch.

122

Then one day, imagine his surprise and anger when he found someone else on his land! A hundred men were at work at the foot of the mountain putting up a big bunkhouse and a big cook-house. They did not look like cowboys at all, and they did not have any cattle with them—except for one huge blue-colored ox. He was a hundred times bigger than any steer Pecos Bill had ever seen before, and he had an appetite to match. He ate a whole wagonload of hay at one swallow!

Pecos Bill did not stop to think that he was only one man against a hundred men, and that the huge ox could kill a person by stepping on him. He rode right up to the camp and asked, "Who is in charge here?"

"Paul Bunyan," answered one of the men.

"I want to talk to him," said Pecos Bill.

The man called, "Paul!" And there, striding out from among the trees came the very biggest man in all the world—as big for a man as the Blue Ox for a steer. Now Pecos Bill himself was a fine figure of a man, six feet two inches high, straight as an arrow and as strong and limber as a rawhide lariat. But this Paul Bunyan was so tall that his knee was higher than Pecos Bill's head! He wore flat-heeled, broad-toed boots, not like cowboy boots at all. He wore no chaps, and instead of a leather jacket he wore a queer woolen jacket of bright-colored plaid. His eyes were deep-set and his mustaches were big as the horns of the Bighorn sheep.

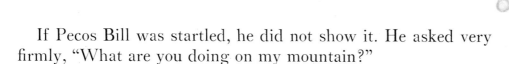

If Pecos Bill was startled, he did not show it. He asked very firmly, "What are you doing on my mountain?"

"This is my mountain now," Paul Bunyan announced. "I've already settled on it."

"That makes no difference. I laid claim to this land long ago," Pecos Bill argued.

"Where's the law that says it's yours?" demanded Paul Bunyan.

"Here it is!" exclaimed Pecos Bill. "This is the law, west of the North Woods," and he slapped his hand on his pistol.

"That's not fair!" cried Paul Bunyan. "I'm not armed. In the North Woods, we don't fight with pistols. We fight with our bare fists or with our axes."

"Very well," agreed Pecos Bill. "I have no axe, but I'll use my branding iron to hit with."

Now the branding iron that Pecos Bill carried that day was known as a running iron. It was a straight bar with a crook at one end. Cowboys heated the end of the running iron and drew letters on a steer's hide as easily as you would draw with a piece of crayon on paper.

Pecos Bill heated the end of his branding iron on a blazing star that he had picked up the time the stars fell. He always carried the star with him, so as to have a fire immediately whenever he needed one.

With the hundred men watching, the fight started. Paul Bunyan picked up his axe and hit at Pecos Bill so hard that he cut a huge gash in the earth. People call it the Grand Canyon of the Colorado River.

Then Pecos Bill swung his red-hot iron, missed Paul Bunyan, and scorched red the sands of the desert. That was the beginning of the Painted Desert out in Arizona.

Again Paul Bunyan tried to hit Pecos Bill and again he hit the ground instead. The scores of strange-shaped rocks that are piled up in the Garden of the Gods in Colorado were split by Paul Bunyan's axe in that fearsome fight.

Pecos Bill's iron, instead of cooling off, grew hotter and hotter, until with one swing of his iron he charred the forests of New Mexico and Arizona. These trees, burnt into stone by the heat from Pecos Bill's running iron, are now the famed Petrified Forest.

Neither man could get the better of the other. For the first and only time Pecos Bill had met his match. And it was the first and only time that Paul Bunyan's crew had seen a man that could stand up to him.

Finally they both paused to get their breath, and Paul Bunyan suggested, "Let's sit down a minute."

"All right," agreed Pecos Bill, and they sat down on nearby rocks.

As they sat resting, Pecos Bill asked, "Stranger, why are you so anxious to take my land away from me? Isn't there plenty of other land in the West that you could have just by laying claim to it?"

"Land!" exclaimed Paul Bunyan. "It's not the land I want!"

"Then why are we fighting? What do you want?" inquired the surprised Pecos Bill.

"Why, the trees, of course," Paul Bunyan explained. "I'm no rancher. I have no use for land any longer than it takes to cut the timber. I'll log the trees off that mountain, and then I'll be through with it. I'm a lumberman."

"Why didn't you say so at first?" exclaimed Pecos Bill. "You are more than welcome to the trees! I've been trying to find some way to get them off the land so that the grass can grow on the slopes and my cattle can graze there."

"They'll be off in a few weeks," promised Paul Bunyan, and the two men shook hands.

Pecos Bill and Paul Bunyan became the best of friends after that, each respecting the other for the fight that he had put up. Pecos Bill and his cowboys delivered a herd of nice fat young steers to furnish beef for Paul Bunyan's loggers while they were clearing off the trees. When Paul Bunyan and his men were finished, they left standing their big bunkhouse and their big cookhouse and the Blue Ox's barn, ready for Pecos Bill's outfit to move in.

Hallabau's Jealousy

A long time ago, there lived a man who had two sons. Although he was very fond of the boys, he longed for a daughter, so that when one day his wife had a baby girl, he was overwhelmed with joy.

Nothing he could do for the baby was too much trouble. Whenever he went to market he would bring her sweetmeats or a bright bauble. But the boys would be lucky if they had new caps for the feast days.

Nor, as the child grew, would she be sent to the bush with other children her age to help gather wood or carry water. Her brothers had to do all the chores.

Time passed, until the child grew into a pretty young girl with bright eyes and smooth brown skin. Her arms and legs were unblemished by scratches such as were seen on other young girls who had to work in the home and help their parents in the fields, amid thorns and rocks.

Now her brothers, Hallabau and Shadusa, grew jealous of the way in which their father treated them, in contrast with the way he favored their sister. Hallabau, the first-born, often lay awake at night, considering how he might get rid of his sister. At last he thought of a plan.

One morning, when the girl was in her eleventh year, the two brothers were told by their father to go to the forest and collect firewood. Hallabau turned to his sister where she sat on a goatskin mat in the shade thrown by the thatched roof of their house, and said gently:

"Come with us to the forest, sister, and help us gather wood. My brother and I will climb the trees and break off the dead branches, and if you will stand below to collect the pieces into bundles, our task will be much lighter. Do not be afraid," he said with a smile, as he saw his sister hesitating, "we will look after you. No harm can come to you if you are with us."

The girl was flattered because her brothers sought her company, and she followed them out of the compound and into the dark, shady forest.

At first Hallabau and Shadusa climbed tall trees and broke off the dead branches, while their sister piled the sticks together and tied the large bundle with stout vines.

"Take this bundle of wood to the edge of the forest, Shadusa," said Hallabau, "and then return for another bundle which my

sister and I will have ready for you."

The younger brother did as he was told, and as soon as the sound of his footsteps was silenced by the forest duff, Hallabau seized his sister and flung her over his shoulder.

"Let me go! Let me go!" she screamed, but he took no heed and began to climb a tall mahogany tree, which he had previously selected for his wicked purpose. The girl lay still, fearing that she would fall to her death if her brother dropped her. Hallabau climbed higher and higher until he reached a thick branch, well hidden by leaves.

Pulling a rope of strong vines from under his clothing, he bound her to the branch of the tree so tightly that she could not move. When the child realized her fate, she fainted dead away.

This suited Hallabau admirably. He then clambered down the tree as speedily as possible and ran along the path that his younger brother had taken. Presently he met him returning for more wood.

"Alas! Alas!" sighed Hallabau. "I have lost our sister. Come and help me find her, or our father will be angry indeed!"

"Which way did she go?" cried Shadusa in alarm.

"She went this way," said the wicked brother, pointing in the very opposite direction from the tree where he had bound his sister.

The two boys searched for several hours, but of course they did not find her. At last they decided to go home and break the bad news to their father. He was shocked and angered, and made the older boy go back and search far into the night. Eventually the father's anger turned to grief, believing that his daughter was lost forever.

Meanwhile, in the deep forest the young girl recovered from her faint, and kept calling loudly in the hope that someone might hear her and set her free. But nobody passed by, and her throat grew parched with heat and thirst.

Toward evening of the second day she heard the sound of men's voices and the gentle footsteps of donkeys trotting along the path below. Looking down she saw a caravan of traders, each driving several donkeys loaded with large bags of kola nuts. Last of all came the leader of the caravan, riding the strongest of his animals and encouraging the men and beasts to make haste, so that they might reach their night's resting place before sunset.

Twisting her head in their direction, the girl sang:

"Oh, do you know my brother?
Have you heard of Hallabau?
He has bound and treed me.
O, somebody save me, please!"

The men stopped in their tracks, craning their necks upward to see who could be singing so sweetly.

"It is a magic bird," said some. "No, it is an evil spirit," said others.

Then the girl sang again:

> "*Oh, do you know my brother?*
> *Have you heard of Hallabau?*
> *He has bound and treed me.*
> *O, somebody save me, please!*"

"It sounds like a young maid," said the leader of the caravan, and he began to climb the mahogany tree until he found the girl, cruelly tied to a big branch. As he loosened her hands, he asked: "Are you a maiden? Or are you a spirit?"

"O sir!" exclaimed the girl, "I am a poor maiden whose jealous brother has tied me and left me to die."

Now the leader was a rich man and a kind one, who had no children of his own, and when he saw how gentle the girl was, he made haste to help her down from the tree, and set her upon his own donkey, saying:

"You must not go back to your father's house, for your brother will only try to kill you again. Come home with me. From now on, you shall be my daughter."

So the caravan went on its way, and when the man at last reached home, his wife welcomed the girl and she lived with them as their daughter for many years, growing ever more beautiful as time went by. People came from far places to gaze upon her, and gradually it was forgotten that she did not belong to the trader and his wife.

When she reached the age for marriage, her foster father declared that none but the best of men could be her husband.

Now all these years Hallabau, her elder brother, had been growing strong and handsome. One day he told his father that he wanted to set out on a journey to find himself a wife. The fame of the girl who was his sister had reached even the small village where he lived, and Hallabau decided to take her gifts and to try his luck as a suitor.

His father gave him fine clothes, a large bag of bright shells, and a basket of kola nuts to take with him. The whole village turned out with drums and songs to wish him luck on his quest.

He traveled several days, asking at different villages how to reach the home of this maiden so renowned for her beauty. One evening as the sun was setting, he arrived at the home of the rich trader.

How handsome Hallabau looked, standing at the entrance to

the compound, tall and upright, his brown skin shining in the golden light of the sun, his gifts lying mounded at his feet.

When the trader heard why he had come, he talked with Hallabau far into the night and at last satisfied himself that here was a young man worthy to be the husband of his beautiful daughter.

Next morning the girl was brought out of her hut, and Hallabau found himself speechless in the presence of such beauty. The girl, too, was attracted by the young man's good looks, but as soon as he found his voice and began to talk, she recognized him for what he was—her elder brother!

She said nothing, but watched him tender the precious gifts to her foster father; then, bidding the kindly couple a sad farewell, she set off with Hallabau on the journey back to his home. During the whole time she spoke scarcely at all, but the young man assumed that she was shy, and thought nothing of it.

Her real parents greeted her with open arms and began to make preparations for the wedding. They did not recognize her as their long-lost daughter and wondered at her silence.

Now when the girl had left her foster parents, they had given her a golden pestle with which to pound the grain to make millet cakes for her husband after their marriage. But she took the pestle from her bundle and began to use it the very evening of her arrival. She poured some grain into a mortar, and swinging the golden pestle up and down, she pounded the grain, singing sweetly as she did so:

"How can I marry my brother?
How can my father be told?
Will even my mother believe me
If I give her this pestle of gold?"

The people in the compound heard her sweet singing and gathered softly around to see the beautiful maiden they had heard so much about, and to listen to her song. Imagine their surprise when they saw her eyes red with weeping, and heard her sing again and again:

"How can I marry my brother?
How can my father be told?
Will even my mother believe me
If I give her this pestle of gold?"

Then one old woman who heard the song fetched Hallabau's

parents, and together they hid behind the mat fence, listening as she sang.

"Surely," whispered the father, "she cannot be our long-lost child!"

"From the first, I thought there was something familiar about her face," replied the mother.

"Well, there's one way to be sure," suggested the father. "Don't you remember that our daughter has a birthmark in the middle of her back?"

"Of course!" exclaimed the mother. "Let us go and ask the maiden about it now."

So the parents went to the girl where she was busily pounding corn with her golden pestle.

"May we please see your back?" they asked. "We think you might have a mark that will prove you are our own daughter."

At this, the girl burst into tears of relief and embraced her parents, saying: "Come, see for yourselves! I am indeed your long-lost daughter."

Then followed such rejoicing as had never before been seen nor heard in the village. Fires were lit and delicious food was cooked; drummers were summoned and everyone danced for joy.

But the wicked brother Hallabau was so ashamed of what he had done all those long years ago, that, taking his bow and arrow, he quietly left the compound, disappearing into the night, and was never heard from again.

Galahad

King Arthur and his knights were assembled at the Round Table. Only one place stood empty: the Seat Perilous, so called because none but the absolutely pure dared sit in it without imminent danger. It stood always covered with a heavy cloth.

On this day an old hermit accompanied by a blond youth entered the hall.

"Your majesty," said the hermit in a steady, sure voice, "I have brought one who is to sit in the Seat Perilous."

"Are you mad?" asked King Arthur. "Even the most honorable of my knights is not without fault. None can claim to be pure enough to occupy the Seat Perilous. Who is this foolhardy boy you have brought?"

"His name is Galahad, and he is a descendant of Joseph of Arimethea. It was Joseph of Arimethea who recovered the soldier's spear which pierced the side of the Saviour. It was the same Joseph who was entrusted with the cup from which Jesus drank at the Last Supper, and which caught His blood when the spear pierced His flesh on the cross.

"That cup," continued the old hermit, holding an imaginary cup in both of his calloused hands, "is the Holy Grail—guarded from generation to generation by holy men. But, alas, as time went by, new guardians grew careless and profane. One day the Grail was no longer there. It is still on earth," the old man said, "but it cannot be seen except by one who is without sin of thought or deed."

King Arthur looked at his knights, but none met his gaze.

"Of all quests, that would be the noblest and the most difficult," the king said. "But what has this to do with the boy? And why do you think he is fit to occupy the Seat Perilous?"

"Because I see what none of you has yet seen," said the hermit, pointing to the chair. All eyes turned his way as he lifted the heavy cloth and read what appeared to him in letters of gold: "This is the seat of Galahad, the pure in heart."

The old hermit nodded with conviction. "The lad shall stay here until he wins the right to knighthood. Then he must leave on his quest to find the Holy Grail."

According to the hermit's plan, Galahad went into training—first as a page, then as a mounted squire—to become eligible for knighthood. He learned jousting; and his tourneying became both brave and bold. His chivalry was unmatched. He could unhorse any opponent without injuring him; he could win without wounding.

Within a year he won his spurs as the youngest knight at King Arthur's court. At last he was ready to set forth on his quest. Every knight, even the most seasoned, pleaded to go with him.

"I thank you all," he said. "But this is something that has been foreordained, and it is something I must do alone."

Many were Galahad's adventures and triumphs. He saved lords from undignified death, and rescued ladies from cruel captivity. He stopped marauders from vandalism, and helped murderers to repent. He overcame every adversary and endured every hardship. His strength was as the strength of ten because his heart was pure.

One night he came to a castle where an old king lay grievously wounded near an altar.

"My wound," he told Galahad, "will never heal. It was caused by the spear that pierced our Saviour's side. Once I had it in my keeping, for I was brought up to be a holy man. But in my early manhood I sinned and the spear fell on me. Then it strangely disappeared. The wound it caused has crippled me. Though I am in constant pain, I cannot die. Only a miracle can save me."

"Do not lose faith," said Galahad. "Know that you have been strong to stand such suffering. Know, too, that your suffering must end. Believe it."

In the days that followed, Galahad could not forget the king and his wound that would not heal, nor the spear that had vanished. He went on, looking for a sign that would tell him his quest was not in vain.

One evening he came to an abbey of white friars and, after spending the night there, he was shown the abbey's sacred treasure. It was a white shield.

"It may look like any other shield," explained one of the friars, "but it has a strange history. Ever since the abbey was founded, the shield has been here. No one knows where it came from, nor the reason for its curious power. Any knight who wears it, any knight except one, will be killed or maimed within three days.

Many knights have laughed at the story and many have put on the shield and gone forth to battle. All have been found dead or disabled within three days, and their squires have brought the shield back. Here it stays, waiting for the one who can wear it without hurt."

"You say that it is harmful to any knight except one," said Galahad. "Do you know who that one might be?"

The friar shook his head. "We do not know. It could be anyone. It could be you."

"It could be," said Galahad. "It could be the sign I am seeking. Let me put it on."

The shield was brought to him with tremulous hands. Galahad lifted it, and suddenly a dazzle of light filled the room. The walls glowed, the windows flamed with quivering colors, and on the white shield there appeared a shining golden cross. Its brightness increased as Galahad hung the shield around his neck and went onward with his quest.

A feeling of forewarning told him that what he was seeking was on this earth but not on land. He struck out toward the sea, and when he reached the shore, he found a ship without a crew but with all sails set for departure. Galahad entered the ship and it took off smoothly for the city of Sarras. There the ship dropped anchor, and a silver table appeared in the center of the deck where nothing had stood before. It was a massive silver table, bearing an object covered with a silken cloth. Galahad felt it must not be uncovered until the appointed moment. A man was standing on the shore, and Galahad asked if he would help carry the table.

"Gladly would I help if I could," said the man. "But I have not walked for ten years, except with crutches."

"Nevertheless," said Galahad, "come aboard and show your good will."

The man raised himself with difficulty, but as soon as he touched the table he straightened, his crutches fell, and he stood up stronger than he ever had been.

News of the miracle spread through the city; it reached the ruler, who was confined to his bed by a disease no doctor could cure. He sent word that, if Galahad would restore him to health, he would surrender his greatest treasure—a spear which had mysterious powers but which no man could lift.

On strong shoulders the table was carried to the ruler's bedside. Galahad sensed this was the moment that had been appointed. He drew away the silk covering while an unearthly light pierced the darkness of the sick room. The light came from a cup on the table, a liquid light that turned from gold to blood-red. Galahad clasped his hands and kneeled. He knew this was the precious vessel, the Holy Grail, and he knew that he had come to the end of his quest. He bent in adoration while the Grail rose from the table, hovered above his head, and ascended to the skies. He did not notice the king, who had left his bed and stood transfigured with joy.

"Stay here!" cried the ruler. "You have performed a miracle! Sarras is yours!"

"We have had a revelation," Galahad answered. "I can only surmise what it may mean, but I know I am not meant to stay in Sarras. I have been brought here to further my mission. You spoke of a spear. If I can carry it, let me try."

There was no need for Galahad to lift the sacred weapon. It floated toward him and fitted itself into his hand as if made for him alone.

The journey back was swift. The ship was waiting, the paths on land seemed to straighten themselves for his passing, nothing opposed his progress. He entered the old king's castle and, without a word, touched the king's wound with the point of the spear. The wound healed on the moment, and the king enfolded Galahad in an embrace that was also a worship.

In good time Galahad returned to the court of King Arthur. He placed the sacred spear upon the altar, his quest fulfilled. He had seen the Holy Grail and had earned the right to sit in the Seat Perilous. Pure and peerless, he became the fabled hero, the perfect knight—Sir Galahad.

momotaro

Long ago in Japan there lived an old man and his wife. One day the old man went to the mountains to cut wood, and the old woman went to the river to do her washing. As she rubbed and scrubbed, a peach came floating, *tsunbura tsunbura*, down the river. The old woman plucked it from the water and when she tasted it, found it to be delicious.

"This peach is so good," she thought, "I'd like to take one to my old man too." So she called out, "Good peaches, come this way; bad peaches, go that way." Soon a large, delicious-looking peach floated into the old woman's hands. "This one looks good," she cried, and picking it up, she carried it home and put it in a cabinet.

When evening came, the old man returned home from the mountains with a load of wood on his back. "Old woman, old woman, I am home," he called.

"Old man, old man, I brought you a delicious peach today from the river. Here, I've saved it for you to eat." And she brought the peach from the cabinet.

Just as she put it on the cutting board to cut it open, it suddenly split apart. Inside was a beautiful baby boy who began crying lustily, *hoogea hoogea, waa waa.*

The old man and his wife were overcome with surprise and made a great to-do, crying, "Oh, oh, what shall we do?"

"Since he was born from the peach, let us name him Momotaro (Peach Boy)" they said; and so they did. They raised him very carefully, feeding him rice gruel and fish. He would eat one bowlful and grow that much bigger, and if he ate two bowlsful, he would grow that much bigger. If he were taught to count to one, he could remember all the numbers up to ten. He grew to be a strong and intelligent boy. The old man and his wife loved him and took great pleasure in caring for him.

One day Momotaro went to the old man and his wife. He sat down on the floor in the formal style, with his hands on the mat before him, and said, "Grandfather and Grandmother, I am grown now; I should like to go to the Oni Island and conquer the wicked oni. Please make some of Japan's number-one *kibi dango* (pounded rice and millet dough) for me."

The old man and his wife tried to dissuade him. "Why do you ask to do this? You are not old enough; you could not defeat the oni."

Momotaro, however, said, "I shall defeat them." He would not be dissuaded, so the old man and the old woman could do nothing but agree.

"Then you may go and do it," they said, and they made a great panful of Japan's number-one *kibi dango*. They tied a new towel about his head and gave him new *hakama* (wide trousers). They gave him a sword and a flag upon which was written, "Japan's Number-One Momotaro." Tying a bag of *kibi dango* to his waist, they said, "Be careful. Go and return. We will wait for you until you have conquered the oni."

With the blessing of the old man and his wife, Momotaro departed. He went as far as the edge of the village when a dog came barking up to him, "*Wan wan,* bow wow, Momotaro, Momotaro, where are you going?"

"I am going to the Oni Island to conquer the wicked oni."

"Then I shall go to the Oni Island with you. Please give me one of those Japan's number-one *kibi dango*."

"You shall become my retainer. If you eat one of these, you will be as powerful as ten men," and Momotaro took one of the *dango* from the bag at his waist and gave it to the dog.

So the dog became his retainer, and they set off toward the mountains. Next a pheasant came flying, *ken ken*, up to them. He was given a *kibi dango* and became a retainer in the same way as the dog. Momotaro continued on to the mountains with his two retainers. Next a monkey came chattering up to them, "*E kya kya*," and he too became a retainer.

Momotaro now acted as the general, the dog became flag bearer, and they all hurried on to the Oni Island.

When they arrived on the island, the first thing they saw was a huge black gate. The monkey rapped, *don don*, on the door. From inside came a rasping voice, "Who is there?" and a red oni came out.

Momotaro replied, "I am Japan's number-one Momotaro. I have come to conquer Oni Island; you had better sound the alarm," and pulling out his sword, he made ready to attack. The monkey flashed his long spear, the dog and the pheasant their swords, and all prepared to attack.

The little oni at the gate set up an alarm and fled to the rear of the island. There all the oni were having a drinking bout. When they heard that Momotaro was coming, they shouted, "Who is Momotaro, anyway?" and came out to fight.

Since the dog, the pheasant, the monkey, and Momotaro had all eaten Japan's number-one *kibi dango*, they had the strength of a small army and easily defeated the whole oni force. The oni general fell down in front of Momotaro, his hands on the ground, and with tears falling, *boro boro*, from his eyes, he begged forgiveness, crying: "We are no match for you, please spare our lives. We will never do wrong again."

"If you promise that," said Momotaro, "I shall spare your lives."

"We will give you all our treasure," said the oni general, and he surrendered their hoard to Momotaro.

Momotaro put the treasure in a cart, and with the dog, the monkey, and the pheasant pulling, *enyara enyara*, heave ho, heave ho, he returned with all manner of gifts for his grandfather and grandmother.

The old man and his wife were overjoyed and praised Momotaro for his bravery. The emperor heard of the crusade, and Momotaro was given a great reward, with which he cared for the old man and his wife the rest of their days.

ACKNOWLEDGMENTS

M. Evans and Company, Inc., for "Rama, The Bow That Could Not Be Bent," "David and Goliath," and "Galahad —The Holy Grail" from *The Firebringer and Other Great Stories* by Louis Untermeyer, copyright © 1968 by Louis Untermeyer.

M. Evans and Company, Inc., and Pergamon Press, Ltd., Oxford, for "Romulus and Remus" from *The World's Great Stories* by Louis Untermeyer, copyright © 1964 by Louis Untermeyer.

Houghton Mifflin Company for "Little Burnt-Face" adapted from *The Red Indian Fairy Book* by Frances Jenkins Olcott, copyright 1917 by Frances Jenkins Olcott and Houghton Mifflin Company; and for "Pecos Bill Meets Paul Bunyan" adapted from *Pecos Bill and Lightning* by Leigh Peck, copyright 1940 by Leigh Peck, copyright renewed 1968 by Leigh Peck.

J. B. Lippincott Company and George G. Harrap & Company Ltd., London, for "Ali Baba and the Forty Thieves" and "The Emperor's New Clothes" adapted from *The Arthur Rackham Fairy Book* by Arthur Rackham (1950).

David McKay Company, Inc., for "The Black Charger" from the book *Castles in Spain* by Bertha Gunterman, originally published by Longmans Green & Co., Inc., copyright 1928 by Longmans Green & Co., copyright renewed 1956 by Bertha Gunterman; and for "The Master Cat" from *The Blue Fairy Book*, edited by Andrew Lang, copyright 1946 by the David McKay Company, Inc.

Krystyna Orska for "The Basilisk," copyright © 1972 by Krystyna Orska.

Pantheon Books, A Division of Random House, Inc., for "The Three Hermits" from *Russian Stories and Legends*.

Charles Scribner's Sons for "Mimer, the Master" from *The Story of Siegfried* by James Baldwin, copyright 1882 Charles Scribner's Sons.

The University of Chicago Press and Richard M. Dorson for "Momotaro, The Peach Boy" from *Folktales of Japan* by Richard M. Dorson, edited with permission.

Vanguard Press, Inc., for "The Love of a Mexican Prince and Princess" from *The King of the Mountains* by Jagendorf and Boggs.

Henry Z. Walck, Inc., and Oxford University Press, London, for "Hallabau's Jealousy" from *African Myths and Legends*, © Kathleen Arnott 1962, edited with permission.

Frederick Warne & Co., Inc., and Blackie & Son Limited, Glasgow, for "Painted Skin" from *Old World and New World Fairy Tales* by Amabel Williams Ellis.

Index

This typeface is Monticello

The typeface used in *Stories from Around the World*
was originally cast in 1789 by Binney & Ronaldson in
Philadelphia, the first permanent type foundry in America.
It was widely used for thirty years and then ignored.
Then in 1950 it appeared again,
adapted for the modern Linotype machine to set
the fifty-volume *Papers of Thomas Jefferson*,
and for that reason,
named MONTICELLO.

HUBBARD PRESS ILL

Mime
the Maste
Galahad
Little Burnt-Face
The Master Cat
Pecos Bill Meets Paul Bunyan
The Black Charger
Romulus and Remus
The Love of a Mexican Prince and Princess
Hallabau's Jealousy

STORIES FROM AR

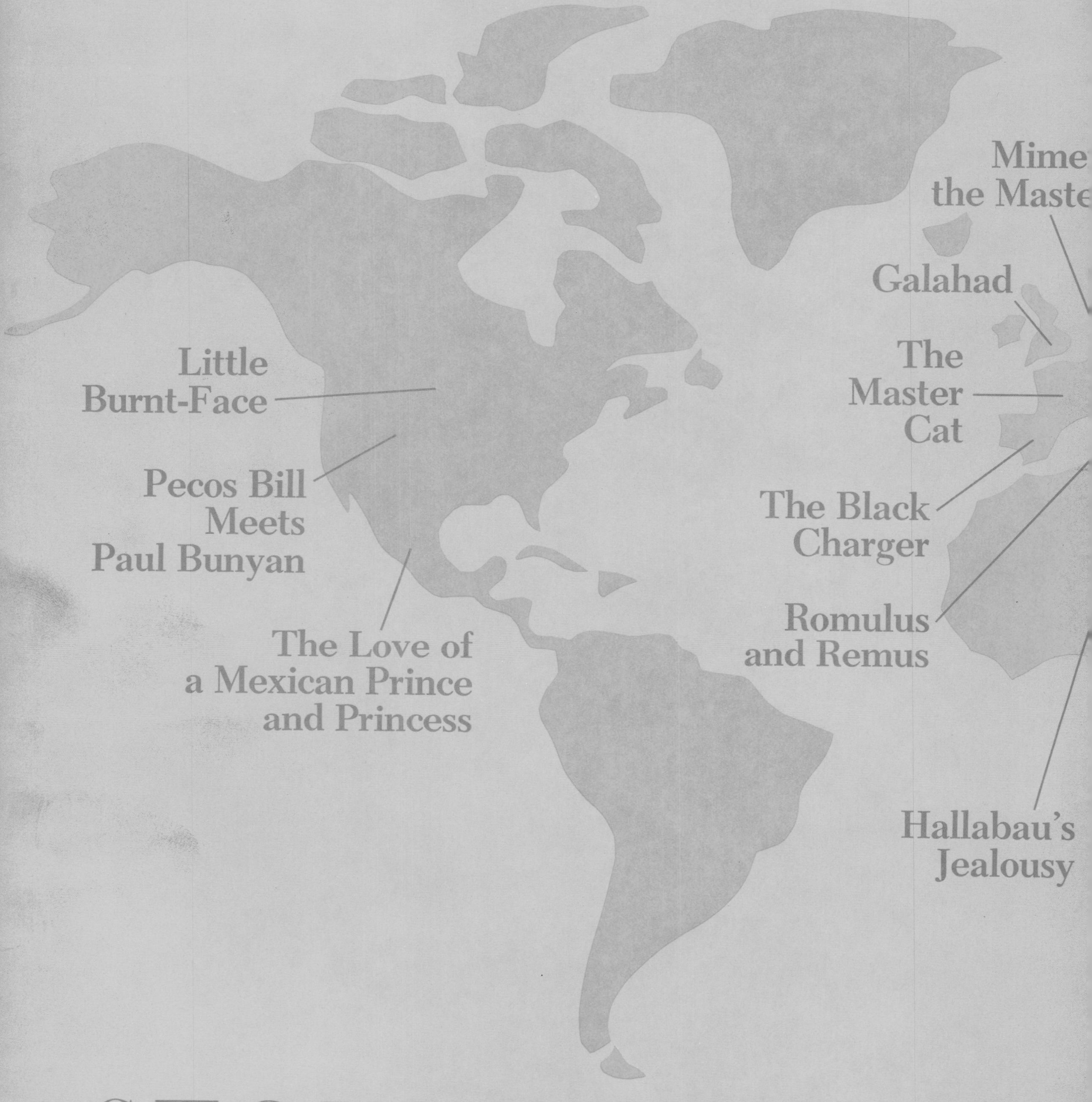